"For those who don't remember, Edward Abbey referred to Albuquerque as 'Duke City' in his novel **THE BRAVE COWBOY**. Harry Willson's collection of short stories entitled **DUKE CITY TALES** all take place in and around Albuquerque. The full diversity of the Southwest is reflected in these eight stories and a novella, that deal with everything from hunting to peace protests. **DUKE CITY TALES** is an interesting first book, a series of vignettes about modern life in the Sun Belt with a quiet sort of intimacy... This book will be of great interest to anyone curious about contemporary Southwest fiction."
-- **John Murray**, THE BLOOMSBURY REVIEW

"The eight short tales and one long one in this book are highly satisfactory. The characters are from Albuquerque, caught up in recognizable situations and dealing with them in convincing though sometimes fantastic ways."
-- **Fern Lyon**, THE NEW MEXICO MAGAZINE

"I think I appreciated the book on the whole for what is left unsaid. You do the Peace Movement a real psychic service by writing fiction like that, that **assumes** much of our common perspective as a given... One of the hardest tasks in working for peace in a world of such overwhelming violence is **believing** in ourselves and in our visions, and your striking shift away from contemporary fiction's usual assumption that violence, oppression and injustice are somehow 'natural' and that anyone who believes otherwise is a 'kook,' **does** make it subtly easier to believe... It really is a rare thing... Keep reminding us that it's O.K. to believe in peace." -- **Rick Miller**, Plowshares Prisoner,
in a personal letter from prison

"There is a troubling question: 'Can a world that keeps needing to be saved be worth saving?' Willson's book is both serious and satiric. It is worth reading."
-- **Herb Orrell**, ALBUQUERQUE PEACE CENTER NEWS

"...The stories deal with subjects ranging from stray dogs to the ethics of nuclear war. Their perspective is mostly environmentalist and conservationist, and their characters are often eccentric, thus reminding the reader of the viewpoint and style of Edward Abbey. In the stories, one meets naive, yet sometimes wise, children, cranks and free spirits, loners and dissenters. Willson's keen insight into human nature is intermingled cleverly within the stories' events, revealing both the stupid and the serious, the touching and the absurd, leaving the reader feeling at the end of each story that he has just been exposed to a truth that he has sensed, but which for the first time is verbalized.

"...The majority of the stories are amusing and unique. Willson takes a colloquial, sometimes crude, matter-of-fact approach to the gravest of society's injustices."
  -- THE SMALL PRESS BOOK REVIEW

"... a delightful tale... a subtle message."
  -- BOOKS OF THE SOUTHWEST

"I can't believe that no local newspaper wants these as a weekly column!" -- WEST COAST REVIEW OF BOOKS

"A curious blend of New Mexico culture, mythology, political statement, and fantasy makes up **DUKE CITY TALES**... The book provides a nice mix of stories for students and adults alike. All stories take place in the Albuquerque area, with settings locals can easily recognize. Regional customs and modern 'folklore' are key elements in each tale... Characters in the stories are interesting and well-drawn... In most of the stories there is a healthy relationship between members of different generations portrayed... Willson reads much like a folksy columnist, using the locale he knows best to sketch creative tales and endearing characters... I like to use the book in Communication Skills classes as a way to incorporate literature and encourage students to write their own **DUKE CITY TALES**."
  -- **Pat Graff,** THE NEW MEXICO ENGLISH JOURNAL

DUKE CITY TALES

Stories from Albuquerque

Harry Willson

Illustrated by Claiborne O'Connor

Copyright ©. 1986 by Harry Willson

All rights reserved, including the right to reproduce this book or any part thereof, in any form, except for inclusion of brief quotations in a review.

Printed in the United States of America
    First Printing, 1986
    Second Printing, 1993
    ISBN: 0-938513-00-1
    L.I.C.# 86-71853

"Ground Zero" appears in
The Spirit that Wants Me: a New Mexico Anthology

                  AMADOR PUBLISHERS
                     P. O. Box 12335
           Albuquerque, NM 87195 USA

Warm thanks to these persons, who helped me find these stories: Adela Amador, Julie Amador, Nicole Amador, Roger Amador, Dean Berenz, Dorie Bunting, Brian Folkins, Armando García, Orlando García, Penny Griego, Mose Hale, Ashby Harper, Harry Herder, Q. N. Huckabee, Mike Kuliasha, Claiborne O'Connor, John O'Connor, Judith Roderick, David Rusk, Andy Willson and Mark Willson.

Other books by Harry Willson:

A World for the Meek: a Fantasy Novel
Souls and Cells Remember: a Love Story
This'll Kill Ya, and Other Dangerous Stories

Other books illustrated by Claiborne O'Connor:

Twelve Gifts: Recipes from a Southwest Kitchen,
by Adela Amador
More Gifts, with Variations, by Adela Amador
The Little Brown Roadrunner, by Leon Wender

Contents

A CHRISTMAS TALE   1
   A boy and his grandfather find new meanings in the luminarias.

TUFTS AND WINK   11
   Games and scores have different functions in two Duke City schools.

GROUND ZERO   17
   Peace protests attract strange people, but who's *really* crazy?

FRONT SEAT   23
   If you blink, you won't see all the bats leaving Carlsbad Caverns.

MOONSET NEAR MAGDALENA   29
   Minnie teaches her father that he can move the moon.

HALF A LOAF   37
   Roger finds what deerhunters dream of.

BALLOON MAGIC   45
   The Balloon Festival can be a time of discovery.

LOYALTY EROSION   51
   The "public thing" and "law and order" do not thrive under abuse.

DUKE CITY ALCHEMIST   69
   A strange old man stumbles on power but is not satisfied with his own attempts to use it. He makes us wonder what we would do with it, and what effect *that* would have on everything.

A CHRISTMAS TALE

"Grandpap, what're luminarias?"
"Who wants to know?"
"I do."
"Where'd you hear that word?"
"Pete told me to ask you if you were gonna put any out this Christmas. But he wouldn't tell me what they were."
"Forget 'em."

Grandpap isn't really as crabby and mean as he sounds. The neighbors and the kids around here all think he's weird --almost like they feel sorry for me for havin' to live with him. I tell 'em he's good to me, and that I'm fine. It's just that he has funny ideas. "He's logical," I tell 'em, but they tell me he's crazy.

"So, what are they, Grandpap?"
"What're what?"
"Luminarias."
"A luminaria is a brown paper sack, one-third full of sand, with a lighted candle inside."
"What's so bad about that?"
"Who said anything about bad?"
"You sound disgusted."
"I am. Stupid idea."
"So, are you gonna put any out this Christmas? That's what Pete wanted me to ask you."
"I am not. Tell that to Pete, or any of 'em."
"Why aren't you?"
"It's stupid."
"What're they for?"
"You tell me."

I've never seen luminarias. I just moved here last summer, to live with Grandpap and go to school here. I get along O.K. with the kids and the teacher, and the neighbors, too. But they seem worried, or something, now that Christmas is coming.

"Grandpap, Pete tells me the luminarias are supposed to light the way for the Christ Child."

"So I hear."

"What does that mean?"

"Ha! He's lost again, maybe. When they ask you, 'Have you found Christ?' ask 'em back, 'Where'd you lose him?'"

"That's not what they mean, is it?"

"No, it isn't. I suppose they mean he's welcome. But who wants to welcome someone who's always on the mean side? Crusades! Inquisition! Obscurantism! Slavery. Genocide. Poverty. Death Penalty. Stupidity! No, thanks."

I'm not sure I know what all those words mean. I'll have to ask him later. I mean, obscurantism? I was gonna ask him right then, but he went on.

"Besides, it's unconstitutional."

"To put out luminarias?"

"No, to force *others* to put 'em out."

"Force?"

"Neighbors try to tell me there's a restrictive clause in the deed to this place. There isn't in mine, though, 'cause I reread it, lookin' for it. They still insist there *is,* that we joined some neighborhood association, automatically, when I bought here. But I *didn't* join anything, automatically or otherwise."

"I heard Pete say they might take it to court."

"Court won't prove anything, either."

"What'll prove it?"

"Logic. And courts aren't logical. Just last year one ruled that crosses and sheep and Latin Christian slogans in Spanish aren't Christian. So all the county trucks still look like Fascist Spain did under Franco."

"You're not afraid of goin' to court?"

"I'm not gonna let court, or anything, make me do what I

don't believe in."
"You didn't put 'em up last year, did you?"
"Of course not."
"Why not?"
"I didn't want to insult all my Buddhist, Hindu and Druid friends."

I didn't know Grandpap had any Druid friends. Wonder who he means. I never met a Druid, that I know of. Merlin was a Druid, they tell me. Then I remembered something Pete said.

"Grandpap, what's an atheist?"
"Where'd you get *that* word?"
"Pete says all the neighbors call you that."
"Hmp. Well, they're wrong."
"What is it, then?"
"An atheist is a person who is ready to assert publicly that he knows for certain that there is no god."
"So, you're not one?"
"I try to avoid illogical positions."

It was a relief. At least Grandpap's not an atheist. But he doesn't seem to care what the neighbors think of him. And they think he's weird.

* * *

I came home from school and found Grandpap arguing with one of the neighbors in our driveway. "I refuse to tolerate such silliness on my property," he was saying.

"Why?" asked the neighbor.
"For one thing, they're a fire hazard."
"We won't put any on your house roof. Just across the front and up the driveway, here."
"I'll have you arrested for trespass."
"Why do you object to them so much?"
"They are symbols I don't believe in, and I'll not be forced."

I didn't know if I should stick around and listen, or not, but I really wanted to know more about it.

"Mr. Jones, we're just trying to hide the dark gap in the line of houses along our street. It looks like no one lives here, on Christmas Eve. The association wants every house lit."

"Yes, I hear there's a competition with other neighborhoods."

"The competition is not the important thing."

"Why all this pressure on me, then? Last year someone tried to put 'em up, even without my permission."

"We never dreamed you'd really object."

"To trespass?"

"So you'll blow the candles out, again, and throw the sacks of sand in the street?"

"It's not funny! It's an unconstitutional attempt to establish a religion! And a very dangerous and narrow-minded religion, at that! Blue laws! Interference! Pious fraud! Armageddon!"

I was afraid it was going to turn into something worse than an argument. Grandpap was really hopping, but suddenly he calmed down.

"O.K. I don't want any trouble. How much is the fine?"

"Fine?"

"I'll pay it in advance."

"There's no fine, that I know of. We just thought all the neighbors could get together --"

"Who do I pay it to?"

"-- and co-operate --"

"I'll pay the man! How much?"

"It costs me about twenty dollars each year, for sacks and candles -- 'course, I put 'em on my roof, too -- and my share of the community sandpile --"

"I'll pay it! Here!"

"It's not the money, Mr. Jones. We just want you to put 'em up."

"That I *won't* do. And don't tell your insurance man, either. Talk about a fire hazard -- on your roof! And all those cars and busses jammed in here, poisoning the air, to see who won the competition -- how would a fire truck ever get in here?"

"I'm sorry you feel that way --"

A Christmas Tale

"It's a bad idea. Bad religious symbols, for a bad religion. Always forcing misery down people's throats."

The neighbor offered to shake hands, but Grandpap was so heated up, he paid no attention. He's not really a mean man, or even impolite, but this luminaria business really has him upset.

* * *

I was already feeling sorry for myself, I guess -- so the teasing got to me. I mean Christmas is pretty close. I miss Mom -- I never realized -- I mean, she has her life to live, too, and the fact that I'm in the world doesn't need to ruin everything for her. So she married that guy -- he never was much interested in me, I know. We all agreed that Saudi Arabia was no place to raise a kid. He makes a lot of money there, I guess, and I'm really happy here with Grandpap. He treats me like a person, not a kid, and I like that.

But the kids at school made me mad today. Makin' fun of Grandpap.

"You live with an atheist!"
"I do not!"
"God'll punish you!"
"That's stupid."
"The Baby Jesus won't come to your house!"
"Oh, yeah? Like Sandy Claws?"

I was losing control of myself. They kept it up, and pretty soon I was so mad I started to cry.

"Whatsamatter? Little Baby Atheist can't take it?"
"Shut up!"
"Afraid of a couple little luminarias!"
"Shut up!!"
"Ya -- ya-ah -- Ya-Ya! Cry, Baby, Cry!"

I poked one of 'em, and Pete jumped in and made 'em stop. I don't know why I got so mad. On the way home I stopped at the sandpile the truck dumped on the only vacant lot on our street. The Neighborhood Association pays for it, each year, and people come and get a wheelbarrowful to put in the bags for the luminarias. I sat in it, and pretended I was at the beach, and thought a lot. Later I tried to talk to Grandpap.

"Grandpap, why do people want the Christ Child to come?"
"There's no such thing."
"What do they want to come?"
"I don't know."
"Why do they put out luminarias?"
"They're showing off. They're irrational."
"Are symbols always irrational?"
"Symbols? I don't know. Why does this bother you so?"
"I'm not sure. Pete says they're very beautiful."
"Hmp."
"Are they?"
"I didn't notice."
"He says a kind of magic comes."
"Nonsense."
"What comes, Grandpap?"
"Nothing."

* * *

I've been wondering about magic. Grandpap is right about the Baby Jesus. He grew up and they killed him, and if he's coming back, then he's not coming back as a helpless baby lost in the snow, anyway. That's silly. The stories say he'll come back as a cruel king and punish people he doesn't like -- I guess I don't believe that, either. I agree with Grandpap -- we're not interested in kings of any kind. Nonsense is nonsense.

But I wonder if magic could be something else. Pete was really trying to tell me something. "It's magic. The light. Something happens. You'll see," he said. He didn't seem upset that Grandpap and I won't put out any. But he wanted to share the magic -- or something. I asked Grandpap.

"Grandpap, what is magic?"
"Magic is the supposed ability to wield powers that are denied

A Christmas Tale

by or unknown to science. Who wants to know?"
"I don't think that's what he means."
"Who?"
"Pete says the luminarias are magic."
"He does, eh? Well, they aren't. They're votive candles in paper sacks."
"I think he said something about the light."
"Well, forget it."
"Said the light was magic."
"I don't see why that entire business interests you so much. There's nothing to it. It's nonsense. Slightly dangerous nonsense. Unconstitutional, but not very serious, nonsense. Unconstitutional wars are much more serious. Let's ignore the luminarias and try and get the wars stopped."

I don't see how a little kid like me can stop wars. Congress can't even stop 'em, if I understand what I read and hear. Maybe magic could stop 'em. At least I'd like to figure it out.

"Grandpap, what's 'The Light of the World'?"
"What do you mean?"
"In one place Jesus says --" Grandpap opened his mouth and raised his arm, but I didn't let him interrupt me. "Lemme ask this!"
"You persist in that silliness," he said.
"You want me to drop it without checking it out? Without seeing for myself? 'On authority,' as you would say?"
"No, not really. So, what's the question?"
"In one place Jesus says, 'I am the light of the world.' In another place he says to his followers, 'You are the light of the world.' Who is? And what is he talking about?"
"I don't know, exactly. Except that *they* aren't. The Christians have been killing people in Jesus' name for ages. Crusades, they call 'em. They're still doing it. Massacres in Lebanon, in Cambodia, and all over Central America."
"The light must be a symbol of something, then."
"Maybe."

We were quiet for a minute. Grandpap was thinking hard,

too. I had the feeling he really *didn't* understand it any better than I did.

"What could it be a symbol of, Grandpap?"
"I don't know."
"Could it be -- what *you* want?"
"I don't know."
"Could it be a symbol of Peace? and Hope? and Love?"
"How could it? A candle in a bag of sand -- don't be silly."

* * *

Pete gave me some candles and paper sacks. I helped him all afternoon, setting out luminarias all over his place over on Fairway Drive. He had these left over, and gave 'em to me. I went for a wheelbarrowful of sand at the community sandpile. I folded the tops of the bags down, like Pete taught me, and filled some of them partway, and put the candle down in -- but I was afraid to set 'em out.

"Grandpap, can I set out a few luminarias? Just across the driveway, and along the front?"
"No. Where'd you get 'em?"
"Pete."
"Why do they interest you?"
"I want Peace, and Love. Don't shake your head at me, Grandpap. I want magic, too."
"You're being irrational, behaving like a child."

Is a ten-year-old kid a child? He treats me like a person, like I said. Almost like an adult. But sometimes he gets so stubborn -- *he's* like a child.

I went back out. The neighbors were lighting candles. It was getting dark. The clouds were low and felt like it could snow, but it didn't.

I walked around the neighborhood. It *was* magic. It was spooky, almost. I could feel the light. It came in my eyes and filled up my head, somehow. Kinda funny -- funny peculiar, I mean. Made the underside of the trees looked strange -- and the paths and sidewalks and walls and roofs winding around -- all lit up and glowing.

"Grandpap!"

"What?"

"Come and see!"

"See what?"

"The luminarias! They're lit -- the neighbors', I mean. And there *is* magic!"

"Don't be silly."

"Come and see!"

"No."

"You won't come out with me and -- and see the magic?"

"No."

"You're mean, Grandpap. There's nothing wrong going on out there. The neighbors aren't trying to be mean. They're trying *not* to be! Why can't we join in?"

"No."

"Why are you so nasty? I don't think *you* want Peace, and Love, Grandpap. Not really."

"That's silly."

"Peace is silly? Love is silly? Then I wish *you* were more silly!"

"Go on outside. Leave me alone."

I went out. I was crying, and didn't know why. I was mad at Grandpap -- but something else was happening to me, too. I sat on the curb and looked up the street at the lights and let the magic in -- into my eyes and into the back of my head, and down into my throat, and -- And I thought of Mom in Saudi Arabia, and I loved her, and stopped being mad at her for leaving me here, even though I didn't even know I *was* mad at her -- but that all kinda melted. And I thought of all the scared burned kids in Central America -- I saw their pictures in some of Grandpap's mail. And I thought of the people living under the bridges right here in Duke City -- and I cried and I wanted to do something about it. And I understood how cross and impatient Grandpap gets with the world, with all its *talk* of love and peace, and all the cruel things we do to one another, and I was sorry I was so mad at *him* just now, and I wished he could feel this magic somehow -- And then I wondered if maybe it would make him feel *worse* because he really can't do anything either about all the pain and hunger and cruelty -- or not much anyway. But we could all do *something* --

I was crying, but I found myself putting my little luminarias out along the front curb. It was dark already, but the light from all the others was enough to work by. I filled the rest of the sacks Pete gave me, and put the candles in them and set them along in front of the driveway.

I was wondering how to light them. Maybe I could light a stick from the neighbors, and poke it down inside the bag and light 'em that way -- I heard the back door open. I didn't look up. I was still crying, but I was somehow happy at the same time. It *is* magic. I kept working at the wheelbarrow. I walked away carrying a sack in each hand. I set them out not far from the neighbor's wall. When I came back I saw Grandpap, kneeling with a match, to light the luminarias next to the wheelbarrow. I stopped and watched.

He duckwalked to the next one, and lit it. He groaned when he stood up. I heard him. He was crying, too. I touched his leg. He wheeled around and grabbed me and hugged me. Then he let me go. We never said a word. He lit the rest of 'em. I set out the last two. Then we stood in the street and stared and stared. When the cars and busses came, we went into the house.

* * *

TUFTS AND WINK

The headmaster told me the day I was hired that the ideal "master" was the teacher/coach. I didn't think too much about it at the time. Besides nouns and verbs and wars and presidents and fractions and binary numbers, I also knew a little bit about football and baseball and volleyball and running and boys. Sure, I could handle a daily "P.E." class.

Before it was over, I was sick of it. Not the fresh air and the running up and down the field blowing a whistle and shouting at the boys. I needed the exercise. It wasn't that. It was the boys' attitude.

We determined sides at random at the beginning of each P.E. class. Count off, by twos. "Ones" on one side and "twos" on the other. Simple. When I saw the boys arranging themselves, trying to minimize randomness, I counted by fours -- and juggled which two numbers would be on one side and which two'd make up the other. That was no problem, really.

It was after the sides were selected that a marvelous thing occurred. A loyalty to the team leaped instantly into play and swept the boys away. Fierce, fighting, raging, slobbering, screaming, bleeding loyalty -- to a team which came into being thirty seconds ago on the basis of how Mr. Green counted and called the numbers.

And Mr. Green was the Cosmic Scorekeeper. "Who's ahead?"

"You are."

"What's the score?"

"Ten to seven."

The attitude of the boys toward the score did not make for excellence of play. I watched for that. It did not enhance skill. I became convinced that it detracted. "Don't worry about the score. Play the game! Play as well as you know how. Learn how better."

But, no. "Who's ahead?"

"You are."

"What's the score?"

"Sixty-five to forty-three."

Later, "What's the score now?"

"One hundred twenty-five to six."

Still later, "Now what's the score?"

"Five thousand two hundred eighty-three to nothing."

"Mr. Green, *Sir!* What's the *score?*"

Other events in school seemed to matter much less. Tests, lunch, fights, faintings, spillings, accidental fallings from ladders, broken windows, explosions in labs, female teachers in tight sweaters -- nothing else captured the emotional life of the boys the way competitive games did. The scores of the games, that is.

The same spirit invaded the charades we played in my English classes. The early works of Tom Wolfe made for good charades titles, I thought -- THE ELECTRIC KOOL-AID ACID TEST, and THE KANDY-COLORED TANGERINE-FLAKED STREAMLINED BABY. I was interested in the words, the sounds, the movement, the acted-out puns. But, no -- the boys were primarily interested in, "Who's ahead, Sir?"

It dawned on me that the boys were learning this strange emphasis from the adults. At a faculty meeting there was a prolonged discussion of a proposal to change the grading system, in some subjects maybe, in the lower grades maybe, from numbers to pass/fail. The upper school English department wouldn't hear of it. They knew how to grade essay papers in such a way that there was a clear and demonstrable difference between this boy's essay, marked "82," and this other boy's, marked "83." I risked trouble by insisting that the difference was unscientific and unreal, artificially contrived by the teacher and existent only in the teacher's head. But in upper school English, the boys could tell -- and even the teachers thought *they* could tell -- who's ahead. Add up the numbers.

"Name a sport that is graded 'pass/fail'!"

Maybe I was supposed to crumple and acknowledge defeat. Instead, I named some. "Mountain climbing. Tight-rope walking. Alligator wrestling. Channel swimming." But they didn't mean that. They meant competitive games.

The faculty conducted a weekly football pool every autumn. A committee put out a sheet with a couple dozen pending football games listed every week. Each participant selected his choices by Thursday and turned in his sheet. A very complicated running score was kept. Pro games, college games, high school games -- from all over the country. Winners of the pool were to be feted at a banquet at the end of the season.

All the interest in ball game scores flabbergasted me. Not national elections, nor hurricanes, nor assassinations, nor crop failures, nor death by plague or car wreck or downed airplanes -- nothing whatever captured the imagination of that faculty the way scores of ballgames did. Monday morning in the faculty lounge was a buzz of names and numbers.

"New York 10, Chicago 7."

"Yeah! Wasn't that something!"

"Rio Grande 54, El Dorado 6."

"No kidding!"

I used to fantasize finding a partner in my heresy and mocking the lounge conversation. Just the numbers.

"Six to four."

"Are you serious?"

"I am. And did you hear about 98 to 14?"

"No! I'll be doggoned!"
"And sixty-six to sixty?"
"I can hardly believe it." But I never found a partner.

I remember one day I was standing in front of the faculty mailboxes. One of the more enthusiastic of the teachers called to me from the far end of the hallway, "Tufts and Wink!"

"Beg pardon?" I called back.

"Tufts and Wink," and he disappeared around a corner.

I stood there, baffled. What was that? I guess I didn't hear it right. Sounded like, "Tufts and Wink." Stuffs and Rink. Duffs and Link. No, it was Tufts and Wink. I opened my mailbox. There was the weekly football pool sheet. I glanced at it, still shaking my head over the incomprehensible message I had just received. Football teams. Dallas vs. Philadelphia. Miami vs. Washington. How do I know who's gonna win? I really don't care enough, that's my problem. Notre Dame vs. Oklahoma. Navy vs. Dartmouth. Holy Cross vs. -- well, lookee here! -- *Tufts!* A college. I've even heard of it. Just wasn't thinking of it.

I ran my finger down the list. Among the high school games -- there it was. Lovington, New Mexico vs. Wink, Texas. They gotta be kidding. Tufts and Wink. I checked them both. I needed all the help I could get in the football pool.

A year later, for lots of reasons, none of them directly connected to ballgame scores, I found myself teaching at a different school. Not the Boy Factory, as I had come to call it in the secrecy of my own fevered brain. A smaller, much less prestigious school. The Girl Farm, I thought, on one occasion, but both schools were going co-ed that year, so my private names were out of date.

My new school was called The Watermelon School. No one knew why. No one had a traditional watermelon story. There was no local watermelon festival. Watermelons were not featured on the school logo, on the stationery, or anywhere. But it was called The Watermelon School.

It was a different atmosphere from what I'd become used to.

A little zany. Here the ideal was the teacher/friend. There was much less so-called "free time" for faculty, and no really "free periods." The kids were all over you, all day long.

Games were an important part of education at The Watermelon School, but with a remarkable difference. In Scrabble®, we didn't waste time adding up the score. We tried to play all the letters, or we tried to make a pattern on the board. We made a list, using the dictionary, of all the two-letter words in the English language. In Spanish scrabble we made lists of all the words played. We used another dictionary to make another list of two-letter words. "Who's ahead?" The group looked up in puzzlement. That wasn't the object of the game.

In volleyball, we had teams. But they were *really* random, as people came and went. Teachers played with the kids. No ref. No score.

"No score? How can you play volleyball and not keep score? What are you trying to do?"

"Keep the ball in the air. Oh, they learn the game. But long volleys are the real object. Correct volleys. We rotate when a point is scored, and the serve changes sides -- but we don't keep track. Doing it is more fun than keeping track of having done it."

The male faculty played horseshoes. We found ourselves keeping score for our games, while they were in progress, but forgetting it as we walked away from the pits. We could not interest the students in horseshoes at all.

We all played softball, but the almost total lack of team loyalty hindered the game. Those people were simply not into scorekeeping. They preferred "work-up." No teams. Get the batter or runners out. When you're out, you become last man in the acres. Everybody else move up. Laugh a lot.

I noticed how rare fights and screaming arguments were. There were no scores to fight about. I was never sure whether the old obsession with the score caused that old all-pervasive boy-factory belligerence, or was the result of it. We certainly had a great deal less of it to put up with at The Watermelon

School.

But, meanwhile, striving to be the best, straining to win, and keeping careful track of the score, has paid off -- in a sense -- over at The Boy Factory. And it was in one of my pass/fail sports.

Last summer the headmaster -- teacher/coach supreme -- became the oldest man ever to swim the English Channel, at age sixty-five. He now holds the record. Fellow never did look his age, or act it on the playing field. Youthful, vigorous, active, strong. And guts. Who's gonna knock it? Not me.

And besides, they tell me that the old Boy Factory has changed, in spite of everything. Letting the girls in did it. Of course, they organized them, too, but the girls had some kind of effect, nevertheless. Hard to pinpoint, they tell me. Just being there, I suspect. Boys can't remain content with game scores only -- not with a pretty girl in the next seat.

Tufts and Wink. Has a ring to it, after all those years. Almost like poetry.

* * *

GROUND ZERO

The wind was raw in front of the Federal Building, where a group of compassionate but helplessly frustrated believers in the sovereignty of the people tried to keep alive our faith in the experiment in self-determination of peoples, by petitioning our Congresspersons to vote against indiscriminate rape and slaughter of persons in Central America who had never done us any harm whatsoever.

Several dozen of us walked slowly in a circle in the space between the main entrance and the three steps down to the sidewalk on Gold Avenue. A couple of policepersons made sure we didn't obstruct pedestrian traffic into the office building.

I carried a sign which said simply, "U.S. out of Central America." "U.S. out of *North* America!" declared a native of the territory we stood on. A fine-looking young woman waved one which said, "Your taxes pay for rape, arson and murder in Central America." Another young woman carried a child and a sign, "You can't hug your children with nuclear arms."

Three or four of us at a time went up to the congressional offices to talk fruitlessly with smiling secretaries and to write notes which they promised to pass on to the honorable officeholders. The printed hand-outs which we received in return for our trouble were so full of distortion and outright falsehood that

I was feeling very discouraged and disgusted, when we returned to the picket line below.
 I rejoined the doleful marchers. A leader called out, "Smile!" but I'm sure we looked a little desperate to passers-by. They must think we're crazy, I thought. I think we're crazy myself. This doesn't do any good. They're gonna go right on murdering innocent people, because they find it profitable to do so.
 The man next to me in the double line carried a sign which read, "Ground Zero." I didn't understand it exactly, but I was feeling so low I didn't react. I gave him a wan smile, and we plodded on around our seemingly useless circle.
 "The world is not as solid as it feels," he declared suddenly, looking me directly in the eye.
 "Really?" I said cautiously, not wanting to be unfriendly, but also not ready for heavy conversation with persons certifiably insane. Funny how these gatherings always attract the unincarcerated crazy, I thought. Helps make the whole enterprise fruitless. He's not dressed in particularly bizarre fashion, though. He could be a poetry teacher at the University, by the look of him.
 "You know any atomic theory?" he demanded.
 "A little," I replied.
 "The galaxy --" and he waved his hand at the sky, "and solar systems and atoms and molecules all consist mostly of empty space. There is very little solid material there, compared to the amount of space. Right?"
 "I guess so," I said.
 "So what causes this sensation of solidness and stuff-ness?" he asked, kicking gently the low concrete wall that separated us from the sidewalk and the people passing by.
 "What does?" I asked in return.
 "Vibrations!" he exclaimed.
 "Oh," I said. Vibrations. Vibes, we called them twenty years ago. Good old vibes. Lotsa *bad* vibes around lately. Vibes that make me discouraged and disgusted, and afraid, even.
 "You from here?" I asked.

"I've been here a while," he answered. "How 'bout you?"

"I been here thirty years," I replied, but I did *not* want to get into any explanation of why I came or what I've been doing all that time.

"Oh! Good job, eh?"

"Not really," I said curtly.

"I guess you wouldn't be here demonstrating, if you had thirty years' seniority at the cannonball factory!"

I didn't reply. His Ground Zero sign caught my eye again as we wheeled around and began pacing in the other direction. "Tell me what you mean by your sign," I said.

"Sure," he agreed, smiling brightly. "Duke City is a prime target, in the event of nuclear war. Did you know that?"

"I've heard tell."

"It's been high on the list for years, as high as third, because of the research at the Base, and now with Star Wars, as those clowns call it, it could move up further."

"So -- I don't get what you're driving at."

"If Duke City is made into any *more* of a target than it already is, sane persons will have to move out, right?"

"I've thought about it. But where can anyone go, where it'd be safe?"

"Is your family still in town, after thirty years?" he asked.

"Not many."

"Where'd they go?"

"Seattle. Rochester. Laguna. San Diego. The Rust Bowl back east. But there's no safe place. Nuclear winter --"

"I know, I know. I've thought of El Rito, or Tahiti. Why do people stay in Duke City, do you think?"

I waxed hot for a moment. "Most people refuse to imagine nuclear explosions in the town they live in. Even the people who make the bombs will not think about it. I used to require my students to do so and to write imaginative essays about it -- and I caught hell from both administration and parents --"

"Well, I for one am making a deliberate conscious decision to stay here, right at Ground Zero. I live over there near the

Base, in that section which is filling up with Vietnamese refugees."

"You don't wanta be a survivor." I'd heard medical professionals talk like that in other conversations.

"No, not that. Vibrations-believers are here," he said, "hindering it."

"Hindering what?"

"The Blast. Just by *being* here." He had a beatific look on his face. In that instant his full beard and brown curls reminded me of the Savior of the World, as some call him. Funny I hadn't picked up that resemblance earlier.

"What's your name?" I asked suddenly.

"Josh," he replied. Josh. Joshua. Same name. And this guy has the same messianic obsession. His presence saves the world, by preventing nuclear explosion, he thinks. The Savior of Mankind. Flesh and blood and hair and eyes and skin and a brain that thinks and decides and --

"And we're getting the job done!" he continued. "See! There have been no nuclear explosions in Duke City, so far! Do you think that's because those mad scientists know what they're doing, and are *careful?* Ha! Or because the believers in the public ownership of the means of production don't know what they're doing, and don't know how? Ha!"

He raved on. I noticed he was wearing tennis shoes. We also have no wild elephants near Duke City. Maybe he thinks he stamped 'em out. He's stark raving bananas, I thought. Off his trolley, off his rocker. Without all his buttons and with a screw loose. Beside himself. Mad, mad, mad.

"Mind power --" he continued. His words fell into my mind like a chant. He *is* a poet, although probably not at the University.

"Impotence at work.
Mind power --
to blind the destroyers
and confound the liars.
Put your body on the line.

Yes, just leave it there at Ground Zero.
Be one who ought not to be destroyed.
Exert the staying power.
The center *does* hold.
'They shall not hurt nor destroy
in all my holy mountain.'
Resist by yielding.
Stoop to conquer.
Go on living.
Deny them spiritual fuel.
Be alive now.
Wield the deeper power."

The group was chanting, and finally drowned him out:

*"El pueblo unído
jamás será vencido."*

Above that chant about united invincible people, he called, "See! It's working! Duke City is still here!"

The chant stopped. "Are you joshing?" I asked him.

"I *am* Josh. My continued existence constitutes ongoing continual joshification." He grinned broadly at me.

Crazy man. But keep it up, Josh. No doubt you're crazy, but so are we. And no slip-ups, Josh, until we get these goddam things dismantled.

* * *

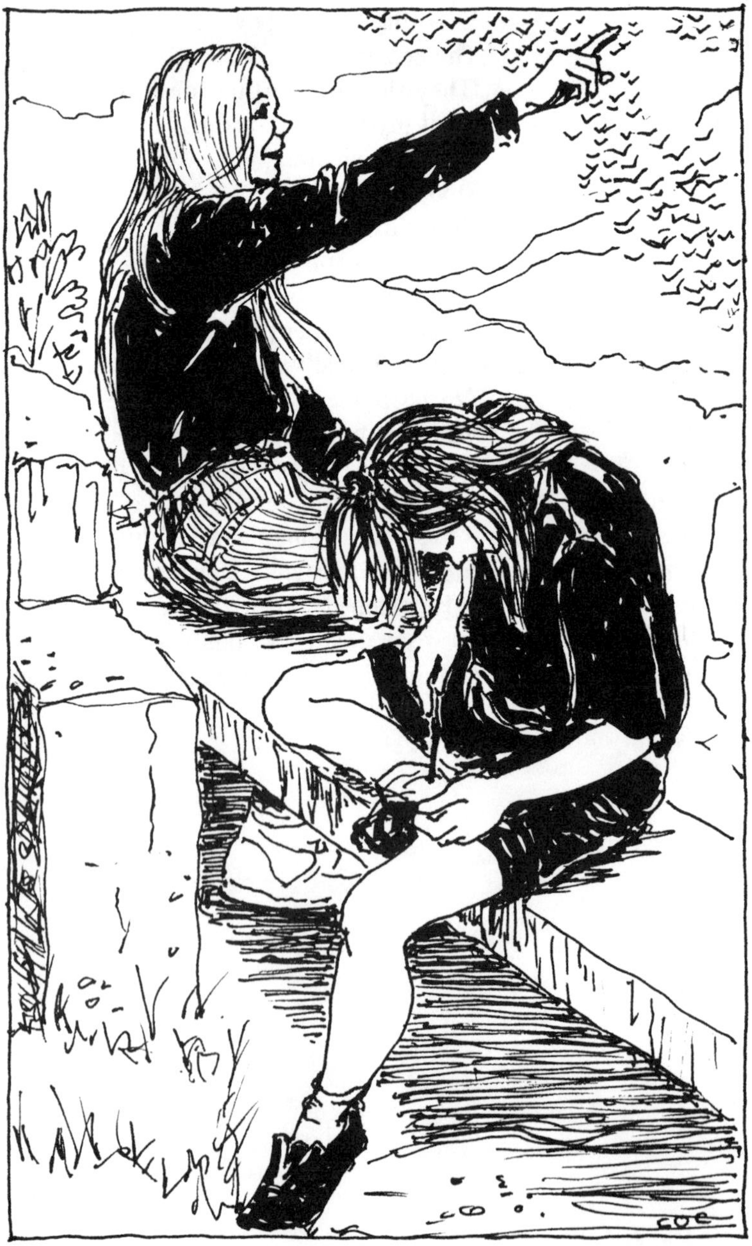

FRONT SEAT

   We drove all day across flat boring country, but Uncle Leo and Auntie Della kept us laughing, with all their jokes and games. The motel is nice, especially that big swimming pool. Uncle Leo stayed in the water with us the whole time. Auntie Della doesn't like the water much, but she told me that Nicole and I were her and Uncle Leo's favorite nieces. That felt good.
   After supper we drove in the car for another hour. It was flat, too, until just the last part. We turned into a crooked National Park road and climbed up and down some. There was a lot of traffic.
   We parked over in the big parking space and walked down here. And here we are, sitting in front of a huge hole in the ground, the entrance to Carlsbad Caverns. Tomorrow we'll all go down in there, Uncle says. I don't know what to think about that. I'm always excited about seeing new things, and I've already seen some interesting pictures of the cave, but going down into that hole in the ground isn't exactly my idea of fun.
   More and more people are coming, filling up these concrete and stone benches cut in a circle in the hillside, like a little amphitheater, across from the cave entrance. Nicole is jiggling up and down, like she does when she's excited -- she's such a little kid. "Where should we sit? Will we see everything from

here? Should we move over there, so we're a little closer?"

I think seeing how many more people are still coming puts her in her little panic. "Oh, let's move to a better seat!"

So the four of us get up and climb up several rows and work our way to the left a little, and sit. Uncle asks, "Is this better?"

Nicole looks around. "I don't know. I think so."

"How is it better?" he asks.

Nicole doesn't know what to say. I think maybe Uncle is annoyed, but then he winks at me.

Some boys, and then some adults, begin climbing around on the rocks beside the hole. They're right across from the amphitheater, and I wonder if they're really looking for special seats, or just showing off. It's hard for us to notice anything but them. One of them kicks a loose stone and it rolls down and falls out of sight into the hole. Uncle is fuming at them, and growling at us, "Why can't they sit here in the place provided?"

Nicole makes us move again, all the way over to the side of the amphitheater next to the stone wall there. She stands, leaning over the wall.

A ranger in a brown uniform and a funny round-brimmed hat comes and makes the people get off the loose rocks. "The United States government has built seats for you. They are over here." As if they hadn't noticed where several hundred of us are sitting. "The tenants of the area you are in may not appreciate your presence. The cactus and the scorpions and the desert rattlesnakes have full run of that area." The word "rattlesnake" moves them. "You people leaning on the wall must find seats," orders the ranger, waving at Nicole and the others. "This is a good crowd this evening, but there are still plenty of seats."

Nicole leaps, arms flying, and lands next to me, bumping me in her hurry. She's embarrassed. She looks around at all the people who are still coming over from the parking lot. "Maybe we should move up there," she says, pointing to the top row of the amphitheater.

"Wanta move?" Uncle asks me.

"No," I say.

"Me neither," he says. "You can go, if you want to, Nicole." But she doesn't move.

The ranger starts talking. All about the Mexican Free-tailed Bat. He talks on and on about bats, more than anybody really wants to know, I think. They go south and west of here, into Texas, to feed. Each one eats half its weight in insects daily. That is, nightly. They come out at dusk -- that's what we're here to see. The Bat Flight. They eat all night and come back at dawn. They hang upsidedown in a special room inside the cave all day. Visitors to the caverns are not allowed to go where the bats are hanging and sleeping during the day. The bats spend the winter in Old Mexico. Just after the cave was discovered, some men used to mine the bat droppings, for fertilizer, but that's not allowed now. Lots and lots of information like that.

"How many of them are there now?" Uncle asks the ranger, when he opens it up for questions. The ranger is ready for the flight to begin, but he can't make it start.

"We estimate about two hundred thousand."

"Is that all?" Uncle exclaims. "When I came here as a boy, there were three million."

"Yes, their number is diminishing. DDT is very hard on them. The birth and nursing of the young is hindered by the poison. Remember, bats are mammals. And they're still making DDT here and spraying it in Old Mexico."

I'm sure Uncle remembers what's a mammal and what isn't. Just this afternoon he was kidding *me* a little about turning into an obvious mammal lately...

And then we smell something. A musty barnyard. An ancient fertilizer mine. You know. *That* kind of smell. But not a familiar flavor, if I may put it that way. I mean, not cow or horse or dog, or human. I'm thinking like Uncle Leo now.

The ranger asks us all to be quiet, so we can hear them, too. The smell is stronger. And then we *can* hear a soft fluffy fluttering sound, and then we see the first of them, flying around in circles at the entrance to the big hole, climbing up in spirals to where we are, to where we can see them silhouetted against the blue sky. Lots of them, circling around and around, up and up, out over the wall, where Nicole was, around and around, higher and higher and then the leaders suddenly flap away over the top of the rocks where those stupid people were, and they fly away, climbing higher and higher as they leave. After a while they form into a long trail of black specks, flapping and flopping and wobbling after one another in the sky, heading off away from the sunset.

I look back at the hole. They are still coming, more and thicker and faster. The sound is louder and the smell is stronger. I try to focus on one individual bat at a time, but it is hard. They fly more like butterflies than birds, I think. Yes, they're mammals, I know. They fly like mammals. Flying mice, they look like, in pictures up close. But now they are a flying cloud. I watch the trail of them waving and fluttering away in the sky -- hundreds of them -- how do they know where they're going? Will they eat too much DDT tonight?

I'm thinking like that, and Uncle asks Nicole, "How's the seat?"

Nicole isn't even watching the bats at the moment. They've been flying for ten minutes, and she's picking a piece of bubblegum off the bottom of her shoe. She looks up at him. "Oh. It's O.K."

"You see the bats O.K. from here?" he asks.

"Uh -- yeah. Sure."

I laugh. We sit there and watch and listen to the bats fly out of the cave. Uncle takes a couple of pictures. Nicole becomes a little bored, which is just like her. And her fussing over front seats, or best seats, or whatever, becomes funnier and funnier to me.

For more than half an hour two hundred thousand bats, which seem like ten million to me, fly out of that cave in a cloud. You will see them. You can't not see them, or smell them, or hear them, if you're in the vicinity.

You will not see them all. You'll look away -- at

Front Seat

your bubblegum shoe, or the little setting thingies on your camera -- or you'll *blink!* -- and miss dozens, thousands. I feel obligated to try to see them all, and find it hard. I give up, and look at Auntie, and smile, and watch Nicole fussing, being bored again, as usual. Her problem is not that we finally ended up in the wrong seat. The seat is not in any way the problem.

Uncle looks sad. "What's the matter?" I ask.

"They're thinning out already. There aren't near as many as there used to be. I hope what happened to the buffalo doesn't happen to them."

"Me, too," I say. Still seems like there's plenty, to me. The sky is much darker, but I can still see that wavering cloud of flying mammals, heading off toward the horizon.

* * *

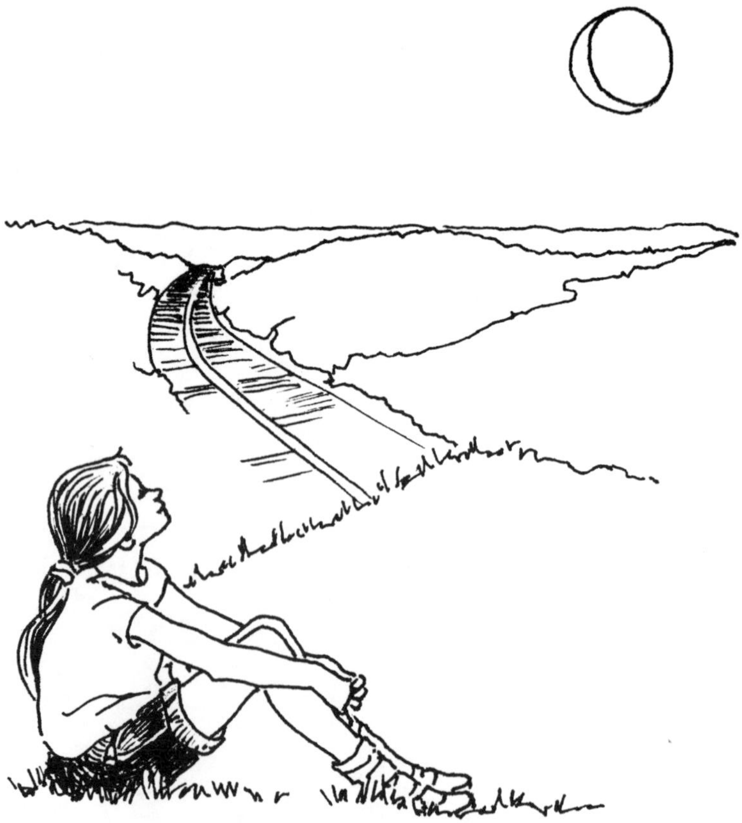

MOONSET NEAR MAGDALENA

Minnie rode in the front seat with her father as they headed west out of Socorro. They had just finished a late morning breakfast, after getting up very early to visit the bird sanctuary down by the river. Minnie enjoyed all the geese and ducks and cranes, but her father seemed sad.

She hadn't seen him for several months, since his visit at the beginning of summer, and now they were going to Phoenix for the long Labor Day week-end with her grandmother. But he seemed so sad, he hardly noticed the birds.

As the road climbed up from the river valley bottom, Minnie watched the bare rock mountains ahead and was a little startled when her father asked suddenly, "Aren't you sleepy?"

She turned her large frank eyes over toward him, and said, "No. Why do you ask?"

"You were restless last night."

"Oh, yes. I got up a couple of times." They had spent the night in a motel there in Socorro, in a big room with two double beds. Minnie hadn't realized that her father was awake at all. "I saw the moonrise," she told him.

"Oh," he said, and added no more.

Minnie remembered waking, feeling strangely excited. She went to the bathroom, and then instead of going straight back to bed, she went to the window and opened the drape partway. She saw a strange glow behind the mountain in the east. She leaned on the arm of the heavy chair there at the window, and studied the mountain. The sky was very dark blue, almost black, and clear. Millions of stars were out, except at the edge of the mountain, where that glow brightened.

It excited her when a slice of silver first poked its way up from behind the mountain. She stared at it as it climbed up further. You can stare at the moon without hurting your eyes, she thought. The moon was very bright, but not a perfectly round silver circle -- part of it was peeled off on one side. But Minnie could see the rest of the circle, much fainter, when she studied it closely. As the moon climbed up away from the mountain, it seemed to get a little smaller. Moonrise. It looks biggest, just as it rises.

Minnie was the kind of girl who does well in school -- she was good at memorizing what they wanted you to memorize. But she often questioned what she learned. The moon doesn't really rise, she thought -- the earth spins. But we still say "moonrise." For a moment as the big lopsided silver ball was looming into view from behind the mountain, Minnie sensed that she could feel the earth moving, turning toward the moon and under it, *letting* the moon appear to come up. Ha! she thought, maybe the earth *does* move.

"You were up very early, too," her father said. Minnie felt he was trying to make conversation -- as if he sensed her awareness of the sadness that kept him so out of it at the bird sanctuary.

"Yes, it *was* early, I guess. But I'm still not sleepy," she added. Poor guy, he's trying, Minnie thought. But her mind went back to the motel room. She remembered going back to bed after her moon meditation. She must have fallen asleep. But she was aroused early, because she forgot to close the drape, and daylight woke her.

Minnie got up, just in time to see the sun rise, too. She had never thought about watching the moon and the sun rise from behind the same mountain. Riding in the car, she thought, "It must happen all the time, I just never noticed. Wonder if Dad ever did."

"I saw the *sun* rise, too," she said aloud to her father. "It was fun to see moonrise and sunrise in the same night."

"Oh," her father grunted.

"Did you ever do that?" she asked him.

"Do what?"

"See the moon *and* the sun rise?"

"Uh -- I don't know. I don't think I ever noticed."

"I never did before, either -- until last night. It was strange. Felt good, but a little weird."

"Mmm-hmm," he mumbled.

The sunrise was beautiful, Minnie remembered. The sun brought out all the colors -- the bright blue sky, the green leaves, the red dirt, the dark blue mountain, and the yellow marigolds in the flowerbeds in front of the motel.

She looked at her father. He *is* sad. I wonder why. He ignored the birds this morning, and there were thousands of them. "Thanks for taking me to see the birds," she said.

"Oh, sure," he said and looked over at her and smiled faintly.

"You weren't as excited as I was," she said.

"I guess not," he admitted.

"I'm so glad they're still alive," she went on. "The DDT and the radiation and the hunters --" She stopped. A look of pain had crossed her father's face. She forgot -- he works in a lab where they invent parts for nuclear bombs, and he doesn't like to talk about it -- *any* of it. Radiation -- sometimes the word makes him furious, and sometimes it makes him sad. It was a magic word for him. Today it added to the sadness.

Minnie tried to change the mood. "I think the birds are going to make it. And if they make it, maybe we can, too."

"Make it?" he asked.

"Live! Go on living. Not kill ourselves, and everything else." Minnie was getting excited. "Mama says there are lots of people --" She stopped again. "What's the matter?" she asked.

Her father was almost ready to cry. He didn't answer. Another magic word? Mama? She hadn't noticed that one before.

Minnie decided not to talk for a while. *I wonder what's the matter with him. He looks so sad. Maybe he's still in love with Mama. If so, he'll have to forget that. It was his idea to break it up. Just because what he thought he wanted didn't work out. Mama finally got over it, and she's found Jim now and they're really happy -- and it's too late, and Dad'll just have to go on without her.*

The terrain they were coming into captured Minnie's attention. The road wound around some as they climbed the crest of a long hill. On top the grass was taller and thicker and there were fewer places where bare purple rocks and bare red earth showed. Black cows were grazing, off in the distance on the right side of the road. The land was flat in that direction as far as Minnie could see. On the left side of the road, south of the highway, a long row of jagged rock mountains extended all the way to the far horizon in the west.

"Oh, Dad, look!" exclaimed Minnie suddenly.

"What?" he asked. She looked into his face and was relieved that he had recovered a little from his earlier mood.

"The moon! Look! There's the moon in the middle of the day." She pointed, excited. The moon was there all right, 'way ahead of them, hanging out over the highway, more than halfway down. The peeled-away part of the circle seemed to be on the other side now, Minnie noticed. "I saw it come up. And now we see it again."

"Yes, that's nice." Minnie wished she could infect her father with her enthusiasm. And she was full of questions. "Why is it there in the daytime?"

Her father was a scientist, full of facts and information. He had a good memory for things learned a long time ago, too. He looked at her carefully before answering. "I guess it must be there in the daytime all the time -- that is, half the time. I mean, it's out of sight, on the other side of the earth, half the time.

When it's on our side, it doesn't matter if it's day or night."

"I don't think I ever noticed it in the daytime before," said Minnie, clasping her hands and gazing at it. "It's beautiful." She noticed him glance up at the moon, and then quickly back to the road.

"If you say so," he said.

"Is that what we call full moon, Dad?" She was pretty sure it wasn't, but wanted him to talk.

"No," he said. He thought a moment, figuring it out from what he remembered. "Full moon rises at sunset, and sets at sunrise. Every day it rises about an hour later than the day before." Minnie studied his face, and then looked back at the moon. "You didn't see what time it was when it rose, did you?" he asked.

"No," answered Minnie. "I didn't look."

Her father looked at the moon, and then at his watch. "It'll set in an hour or so. So it must have come up around midnight."

"Ah," sighed Minnie. "That's interesting."

The road did not proceed westward in a perfectly straight line. It turned for arroyos and cattle fences and outcroppings of grey granite rock. Minnie noticed that the moon was directly above the mountains.

They drove a long while in silence. They passed through the little town of Magdalena without stopping. Minnie was watching the moon all the way.

"It's hard to believe that the moon doesn't move," Minnie said at one point.

"What do you mean?" her father asked. "It moves."

"It *does?* They told us in school that it doesn't. We say it does, when we say 'moonrise.' But it's really the earth that is spinning beneath it."

"Well, that part's right," her father said. "But the moon is also moving, around the earth. Once a month. That's what a month *is*. That's why it rises about an hour later every day. It's really one-thirtieth of a day." Her father was full of information, if she could get it out of him.

"That's interesting," she said and really meant it. She thought about it all, and continued watching the moon. Now it was over the flat land on the right, quite a bit lower in the sky, and looking bigger.

"It's going to set," Minnie said, after a while.

"What is?" her father asked. He had sagged back into almost as sad a mood as ever.

"The moon!" exclaimed Minnie. "Look at it."

"I don't like to look at it," her father said.

"You don't?" Minnie was truly surprised. "Why not?"

"Your mother and I used to look at it," he explained. After a moment he added, "A lot."

"Oh," whispered Minnie. Mama. He *does* have Mama on his mind. Minnie couldn't resist saying something. "You're gonna hafta forget Mama. Really." The pain on her father's face hurt Minnie, too. "I'm sorry, Dad."

"It was all my fault," he cried out, and then he stiffened himself and sucked in a deep breath.

"It's all over now, Dad. And it's O.K. Except you're so sad. You have to let it go -- and forget it."

He didn't answer. Minnie went back to studying the moon. It was over the mountains again. "Where do you want the moon, Dad?" Minnie asked, a little later. There was a slight tease in her voice.

"Where?" he asked, perplexed. He looked at it.

"Over the mountains?" she asked. "Or over the flat?" she added, pointing out over the grassy plain.

"I don't care," he said.

"Oh," she said brightly. "Well, if you don't care, then that's the end of it." She fell silent.

He looked over at her. She stared at the moon a long time and then glanced over at him out of the corner of her eye. "What're you getting at?" he asked.

"You can move the moon," she said, and winked at him.

"What do you mean?" he asked, really puzzled.

"Can we stop here, somewhere, Dad, and get out and watch it set?" asked Minnie. "Or let me watch it, anyway? Please."
"That moon's really getting to you, isn't it," he said.
"Can we stop?"
"Sure, if you want to." A huge cottonwood tree grew beside the road on up ahead. As they neared it, the road began a wide curve. Beneath the tree was a picnic table and a parking place, with no people.
"That'll be perfect, Dad!" Minnie exclaimed. "Let's stop!"
He pulled in. Minnie got out and ran into the ankle-deep grass beyond the picnic table. She flopped herself down and sat and stared at the moon. It was out over the flat land again. "Just look at it," she murmured. She patted the soft grass beside her and said to her father, "Sit here and look at it."
"I'm not used to looking at the moon in the daytime," he said, but squatted down beside her.
"Neither am I." She kept her eyes on the moon. It looked even larger as it neared the horizon. "Sit with me."
He sat. He watched it. They stared at it long enough to be able to tell that something was moving. "Minnie --" he started to say.
"Sometimes I can feel the earth move," she murmured.
"Minnie, what did you mean when you said I could move the moon?" he asked.
She looked into his face. "You *were* moving it, Dad. But you weren't paying any attention."
"I don't understand," he said.
She looked into his eyes. Then she looked back at the moon. "When we were driving along, I noticed. Sometimes the moon was straight ahead of us, right over the highway. Sometimes it was over the mountains. And sometimes, like now, it was 'way out over the flat part." She waved her hand across the prairie. "You were moving the moon."
"I was driving the car." He paused, and then added, "Down the road."
"Yes," said Minnie, and added no more.

"The road was changing directions," he explained.
"That's right," said Minnie softly.
"More than I realized, evidently."
"Right," agreed Minnie.
"That doesn't mean I moved it. The moon --" He paused again. "I changed the perspective --" He stopped. Even scientists catch on sometimes.
"You can move the moon, Dad," said Minnie softly. "If you want to."
He took it all in. "Go on down the road," he said, mostly to himself. "Change directions. Change perspective." He put an arm around Minnie's shoulders. They watched the moon. It was not quite touching that magic line which was the rim of the earth. "Thanks, Minnie," he said softly.
They sat in silence. As the moon touched that edge, Minnie said, "There's another way you can move the moon, Dad."
"Oh? How?"
"Let time pass."
"That doesn't move it," he said.
"Sure, it does," insisted Minnie. "Watch." The moon was hiding, little by little, settling behind that rim.
"I mean that doesn't mean I moved it," he said.
"You find it moved," Minnie said. After a moment she repeated, "Let time pass."
"I can't stop it," he admitted, a little desperately.
"I know. But you can *let* it." Minnie leaned her head on her father's shoulder, as the last sliver of the moon dropped behind the long flat line that was the edge of the world. He held her, squeezed her shoulders, and felt something loosen in his chest for the first time in a long time.
"Thanks, Minnie," he murmured. After a while he squeezed her gently again and said, "Let's go on down the road."

* * *

HALF A LOAF

    Roger stood beneath the sixty-foot ponderosa pines near the rim of the canyon and kicked the hard mixture of clay and pine needles at his feet. Caked solid, no tracks here, he thought, gazing westward into and then beyond the canyon. On the far rim the trunk of a huge pine that had been killed by lightning jutted cruelly into the clear blue sky.
    The other guys said they'd be headed here. Got mine already yesterday, nice eight-pointer. Thought I'd stay in camp today and take it easy in the sun. Clean up, maybe cook something special, like biscuits, only we're outa flour. Sure glad I got one. Old lady bitches less. Pretty expensive recreation otherwise.
    Morgan'll never get his. He's so dumb, and I can't teach him, can't explain it to him. Every year I shoot two and he tags one of 'em. Guess that's why I came out by myself today after all. Get one for Morgan.
    He started down the clay bank, angling a little to his right. There was no trail, but the clay surface was almost bare. Aspen stood below in the bottom of the canyon. Their leaves were down and their white trunks stood erect like poles. Musta been some sight here a month ago, with all that bright yellow.
    The man stopped. He heard a rustling in the downed leaves, then a crashing. He pressed the safety on his 30.06 and raised it to his shoulder. He held his eye away from the scope, waiting

to spot what was creating the leafy racket. But he saw nothing -- no deer, no bear, no man. What the hell?

He inched his way down the canyon side, staying away from fallen leaves, heading toward the noise. Several aspen trunks standing close together in a patch of scrub oak brush blocked his view of the source of the commotion. He held his rifle ready as he skirted the clump of oak. Then he burst into loud laughter. Two fat grey squirrels sprang away from each other and scrambled up an aspen. From high in the air they scolded down at him while he filled the canyon with laughter.

Scared the deer away with all that, probably, but, hell, it's different when you already got yours. He chuckled again. Sure as shootin', squirrels *do* copulate, or there wouldn't be any.

He was down on the canyon floor. He sighted the lightning-blasted tree on a pinnacle towering over the canyon from the far side. He turned at a right angle away from it, up the canyon. Just make a little loop around. Maybe meet the guys later. Or we'll hear each other shooting.

Scrub oak bushes grew shoulder high so thick on the canyon floor he had trouble passing. Recently fallen leaves lay almost ankle deep around their gnarled and flimsy trunks. Twice Roger climbed around on the hard clay sloping walls of the canyon. He moved nearly two miles and saw or heard no game.

The walls of the canyon became steeper and turned to grey granite. The canyon itself became narrower, reminding him of the street of a big city. Wall Street, maybe. A stream dribbled through the bottom. He came to a bright green mossy patch where the sun shone brilliantly. He leaned on the west wall in the sun, studying the emerald color and the flashing water. He bent down to drink, but raised his head before touching the water. Strange smell. He flared his nostrils. Got a good smeller. Something sweet, out here in the Pecos. Sweet, but not clean. Stale, sick almost.

He stood and walked up canyon without drinking. The granite walls showed vertical stripes of white quartz. He thought of the geology he had learned from ranger guides on summer

Half a Loaf

vacations in National Parks. Rocks laid down in horizontal layers, then twisted and folded, and completely up-ended here, by pressure. Pressure, hell -- earthquake, it musta been.

Strange smell again. He turned and looked back down canyon. On his left he spied a space between the sheer vertical rocks, like a little room, or a closet. He strolled to it. Just a fold in the rock curtain. Wide as a man. Morgan would barely fit. He spotted a few brown hairs on the jagged edge of the granite. A deer could squeeze in. Tracks in the sand, not fresh. Yesterday's maybe.

The man stepped into the fold. It doubled on itself quickly twice and became a passageway. Same strange sweet smell, stronger maybe. Probably something died.

He stepped through into an open space and stood in a little virgin valley. A stand of aspens filled the far end fifty yards away. Grass grew in front of him, like a lawn that needed mowing. The grey walls were nearly vertical. He leaned on the wall behind him near the entrance and studied the cloudless sky. Something at his feet caught his eye and his attention narrowed. It was a plastic baggie. Goddam. For a minute there I thought I might be the first human ever in here. Damn litter. He stooped to pick it up and while bent down noticed several more of them, caught in the brush and leaves around the valley floor.

He knelt and looked around. Something strange in that patch of aspens. Something white, beyond the trees, lying down, may not be a fallen aspen trunk. He walked slowly across the grassy patch. More baggies. The white shape was definitely not a natural formation or a growing thing. A box, a shed maybe, in a hidden canyon.

He walked faster and his vision focused clearly on the fusilage of an airplane. The tail-shape was the clue. Reminded him of old airplane models. A body can hardly see what he's not thinking of. Wings torn off. He looked up the sheer walls, and immediately saw what he was looking for -- splintered white shapes halfway up, caught and half hidden behind scrub oaks growing in cracks on the sheer cliffside. A wheel and an axle dangled from the crotch of a towering ponderosa.

The smell was stronger. Oh, my God. He ran to the plane. Half a dozen large black ravens flew away, squawking hoarsely. The plane was open where the wings broke off. Single engine jobbie. Cessna, maybe, but how in hell would I know?

Two human bodies were strapped side by side in the plane. They were badly decomposed. Faces gone. Ravens were helping the process. Rotting flesh there under leather jackets. More baggies lying around.

The man tied his red handkerchief around the lower half of his face, and opened the left side door. He backed away from the stench. Then he pushed himself forward to look into the cargo area behind the seats. White powder was scattered all across the floor, several inches thick in places. Two cardboard cases, advertising sugar in ten-pound bags, lay on their sides, open. Empty and half-empty sugar sacks were strewn around. Bird feces settled over everything, thicker on the seats and the human remains. Two streams of blood, dried and brown, came from under the seats, staining the white powder.

Hafta report this. Beyond the cardboard sugar boxes he noticed a large suitcase. He leaned in and grasped it by the handle and pulled it out and ran back from the wreck. Fresh air. He opened the suitcase and found it empty. He took it to the plane and threw it back in.

He walked around the plane, looking in windows, trying not to study the rotting bodies, but he couldn't help himself. Pale pink skull bone showed where faces should have been. The body on the right had its legs wrapped around another suitcase, a smaller one, like a lawyer's attache case.

The man stepped among the aspen trunks to the other door and pulled it open. The upper half of the body toppled halfway out. The fresh stench caused the man to gag. He yanked the case away from the oozing legs and ran halfway to the entrance to the canyon, where he knelt and gagged again. C'mon, it's just rotten meat. They make baloney out of it.

His head cleared and his stomach calmed down. He opened

the case and his head clouded again. Packs of money. Bills. Twenties. Seven stacks -- a row of five across the top and two below crossways. He took a pack from one stack and riffled one end of it. Old bills. Used money. Five packs to a stack. He began counting. He felt hurried and his fingers fumbled. Why am I in a hurry? Calm down, you idiot.

The ravens were returning. Several landed on the leather jacket at the open door and dipped their beaks in the brown ooze.

He counted to ninety-eight. Probably a hundred in a pack. Five hundred in a stack. He put the pack back and closed the case. Hafta report this. He took a deep breath and walked to the plane, waving the ravens away with his arms. He grasped the leather jacket and its grisly contents, propped them back up in the seat of the plane and slammed the door. He saw human footprints around the plane. Yes, mine. Well, I found it. I *will* report it, later.

He went back to the suitcase lying in the grassy meadow. He knelt beside it gasping for fresh air. He heard a scraping sound near the entrance and stared, waiting. Goddam. Am I gonna lose this? Think, dammit. Don't blow it.

The scraping stopped. He heard a stomping in the sand. Someone coming. A magnificent buck with the largest rack Roger had ever seen strode into view. The animal stopped and studied the man. Holy God. Where's my rifle? It was leaning on the left side of the plane.

The man stood and slowly inched his way to the wreck. The deer moved only its head, following the man's movements. Roger recovered his rifle and sighted the deer in his scope. He had never studied a deer that size that close through the scope before. Doesn't even all fit. A thing you dream about. Heart is there. Brain is there. Beautiful animal. Why is it not afraid? He clicked the safety off and studied the animal further. It lowered its head to graze.

Hard to shoot an animal that is so trusting. Shoot? I don't wanta shoot, not in here. I got mine already. He pushed the safety off, but kept the deer in his scope. He counted for several minutes. Twenty-four points. I've heard of it, but wasn't sure I believed it.

The man lowered his rifle, picked up the briefcase and headed for the entrance. He passed within ten yards of the buck. Let's see. Five hundred times twenty. My God. Ten thousand. Times seven. I'll be damned. And if that buck hadn't come in, I'da forgot my rifle.

He left his hidden canyon and walked further upstream. Hell, skeletons don't need money. The scrub oaks grew thick again, half-covered with their own and aspen leaves. He plunged into a group of them, scraped the leaves aside, placed the suitcase flat on the ground and covered it with more leaves.

He backed up and studied the clump of bushes. Can't see a thing. He looked around. A rock was balanced near the edge of the left rim as he looked up canyon, visible just between two tall aspen trunks. He picked up his rifle and began walking back. Get this damn handkerchief off my mouth. Wonder if I stink. Everything seems to. He knelt and scrubbed his hands in the cold stream at his feet.

He headed on downstream and spotted the "entrance." Sure looked like drugs. Illegal, and crooked to boot, with all that sugar. Expensive business.

He stopped, looking for more landmarks. He spotted three round junipers on the right rim, unusual in ponderosa and aspen country. No one's looking for that plane. He passed his mossy emerald rest stop. The lightning tree was visible ahead. No flight plan was ever registered.

Back in camp, Morgan had no deer. Roger told them he hadn't seen anything. Damn shame I can't tell about that buck. No one ever reported that plane missing. When Morgan threw a cigarette butt into the brush, Roger broke into a furious rage. "Burn the goddam forest down, you fool!" And the others wondered what the hell ailed Roger.

Next morning the hunters broke camp and went home to the city. That night Roger told his wife to call him in sick

Half a Loaf

because he'd be gone all the next day in Santa Fe on special business. He'd explain it to her later.

The next evening he terrified her when he shared his treasure. She hadn't calmed down when he dialed the phone.

"State Police."

"I want to make an anonymous tip."

"A what?"

"I read about 'em. An anonymous tip."

He heard a click on the line and the policeman's voice saying, "Go ahead." Roger hung up.

He went to a pay phone in the new multi-million dollar shopping center.

"State Police."

"Ready with that anonymous tip."

Same click on the line. "Shoot."

"No. A downed airplane. Looks like drugs. Coupla miles northwest of the last campsite on Forest Road 843 in the Pecos. Better hunt by helicopter. Canyon's pretty well hidden. Two dead guys." Roger hung up.

A week later, Roger heard the following announcement on the TV evening news: "A light plane of undetermined origin or destination was found today in the Pecos National Forest, containing two dead and badly decomposed bodies. The plane appeared to be involved in illicit drug traffic, police revealed. Two large suitcases were found in the luggage compartment containing cash amounting to more than one million dollars. Police were alerted to the location of the plane by an anonymous caller, perhaps a hunter. And now, looking at the weather..."

* * *

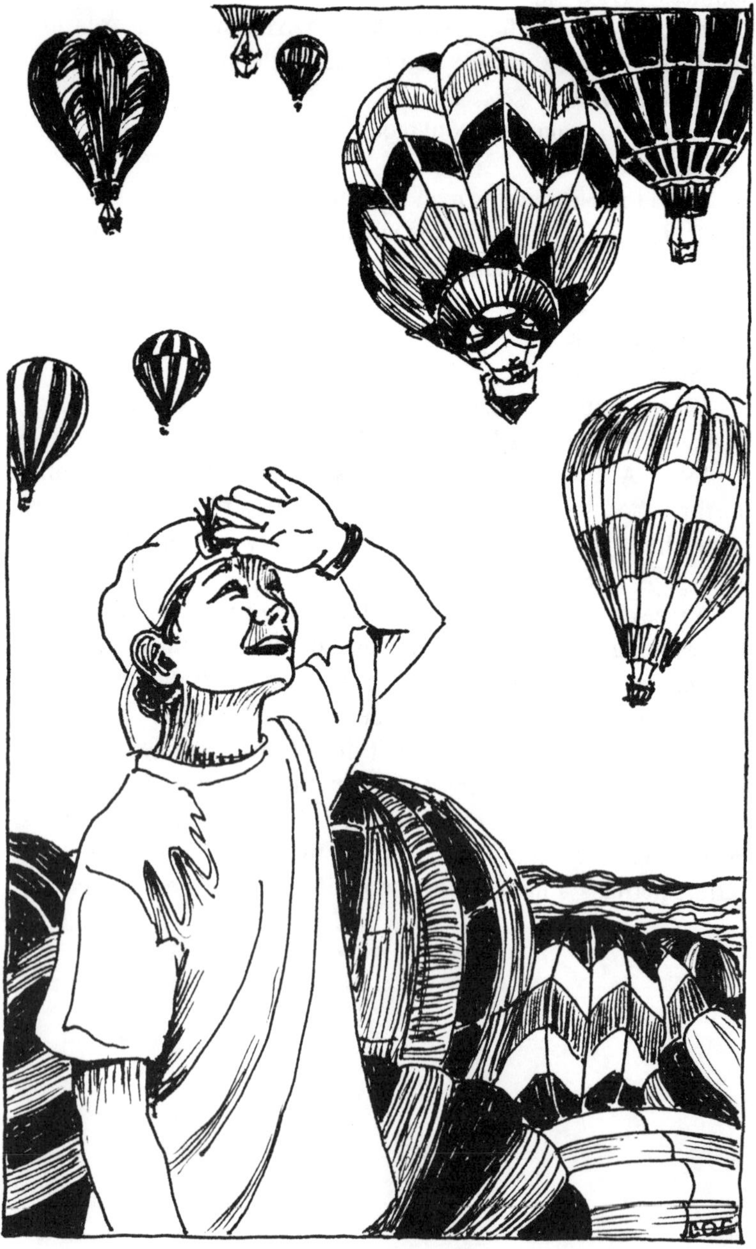

BALLOON MAGIC

"It's foolish and dangerous," Grandpap said.

"Why is it?" I've been aching for a balloon ride for a long time, and now the festival is coming and I've been pestering Grandpap to help me arrange one. But he doesn't like the idea. "What's foolish about it?"

"They're a hazard to traffic. Motorists drive around, looking up in the sky instead of at the road in front of them."

"You're gonna blame that on the balloons? We have hundreds of poor drivers. *You* say that all the time."

"Balloons are a hazard to homeowners."

"How are they?"

"They can't control where they land. They bump into poles and hot wires and trees and roofs. They start fires. People have been hurt in them, and killed by them."

I've read up some on hot air ballooning. Some people *were* killed in the early experimental stages. The wind can be dangerous, I know. That's why they like our good weather here. And the whole idea *was* a hazard to everything, when they filled the balloons with hydrogen. Grandpap can remember the Hindenberg disaster. Maybe that's why he's scared. But things have changed since then. "It's a lot safer now," I tell Grandpap, but he's on to something else.

"This balloon festival is just a trick, a promotional stunt, to bring visitors and their money to an essentially unproductive town."

"Unproductive?"

"What do we make here? Atomic bombs! What useful productive wealth is created here?"

I stare at him a while. "I don't know," I say finally. "But what does *that* have to do with my wanting a balloon ride?"

He stares back at me, and we hold it a moment. I think he likes it that I don't back down right away, like a scared little kid. I *am* a kid, but he treats me like an adult, mostly. As much as he can. His fears and frustrations make *him* childish, sometimes, if you ask me. "Not much," he mutters at last, and breaks into a grin. "I guess I changed the subject."

"You sure did," I say to him.

"This festival, and the hundreds of balloons that come and make traffic dangerous for a week -- it's all a form of advertising. Real estate companies, brands of cars and tires, soft drinks -- it's just a way of calling attention to whatever they're selling."

I don't have much of an answer to that. Some of the balloons *do* belong to those big companies, but not all. "Pete says I'll love it," I say.

"Love what?"

"A ride in a balloon, when I get one. He says it'll do me good. Says it's a kind of magic. It'd do *you* good."

"Not me," Grandpap says, too quickly. I think he's scared. He doesn't want to go up himself, personally, and that's why he thinks I shouldn't. "It's curious to me how often you and Pete talk about magic."

"Really? What's magic, to you?"

"I've told you before. Magic is the imagined ability to manipulate forces that are unknown to science."

"I think Pete must mean something else. Hot air balloons are very scientific. Lighter than air craft. But he insists there's something else, something special."

We let it drop for a while, but I still hope to get a ride when the festival comes this October.

* * *

I've been reading more about hot air balloon flying -- picture books which tell all the history and all the technical details about it. And some old wild and crazy stories -- Jules Verne even wrote one, FIVE WEEKS IN A BALLOON, where they cross Africa. In TWENTY-ONE BALLOONS they cross the Pacific Ocean and barely escape when Krakatoa blows up. But they're all make-believe stories.

And I've been reading about the Double Eagle II, which was from right here in Duke City, and set new world long distance records, and killed its owner, Maxie Anderson, after one of the record flights. Maybe ballooning *is* dangerous, when you're trying to set records. I'm not into that, not now at least. But I *do* want a ride. I want to go up there. Just to feel that magic Pete tells about.

Grandpap and I argue about flying. For all his logic, Grandpap has some strange ideas. No wonder the kids call him weird. Sometimes he raves like a madman. "If you wanta get some place fast, if you live near an airport and wanta go to a place near some other airport, and aren't carrying any baggage, and don't mind flying like a beetle, not a bird -- but then why bother to go? You won't be able to hear any better there than here!" He's waving his arms at me.

I grin at him. "Riding in a balloon, so I hear, is different from flying, like a beetle *or* a bird. It's floating like a feather, not really *going* anywhere. Just being up there, in the peaceful air. I wanta feel that. Floating, drifting, moved around gently by the currents, with no plan, no destination, nothing to prove or accomplish."

"Where'd you get all that?"

"From reading about it. And from Pete. He's got a job as a chaser for the week of the festival. I'm too little, but he thinks

maybe he can arrange something with the guy he'll be working for."
 "I don't like it. I don't want you to get hurt."
 "I'll be all right. *You* should try it. *Pay* for a ride, even."
 "Not me. I'm staying on solid ground."

* * *

Chasers ride around in a pick-up truck, keeping track of the balloon when it's floating up in the air wherever the wind currents take it. The chasers have binoculars and walkee-talkees and sometimes radios -- but they need some hometown people, too, who know the streets and back roads and underpasses and bridges and ditch roads and all that.
 Pete introduced me to Jack, the owner of the balloon he's chasing. Jack's from Oregon. He likes our sunny weather and blue sky. I think he liked me. He said I could ride in the back of the pick-up with Pete and help spot the balloon. Sometimes balloon-owners pay their chasers with a ride in the balloon.
 A funny thing happened when they were inflating this morning. We were at the launch field for the mass ascension. Five hundred balloons, almost all at once. It was a sight -- all the different colors, up in the air, just after sunrise. We could hear people calling from different directions, and then noisy blasts from propane burners. I was all excited, and staring all around.
 Jack and his whole crew were filling his balloon with hot air, using fans and burners. We held the mouth of the balloon open while hot air blew into the big bag. It took a while, but then the bag slowly lifted itself up over the gondola, which was like a big basket, made of basket-material. I didn't realize that I had wrapped the rope I was holding onto around my wrist several times. When the balloon righted itelf, it lifted me right up off the ground. I yelped, and then felt foolish, just dangling there. Jack saw me and leaped up to grab the rope above my wrist and pull me down and unwrap the rope. Two other guys grabbed

Balloon Magic

Jack to add weight and help pull us down.

I thought Jack was a little disgusted, because it took the beauty out of his inflation process. I mean, they had the balloon all cock-eyed for a little while, getting me untangled. But then they took off, Jack and the other two guys from Oregon, and Pete and I and the other chasers rode the pick-up for an hour, and picked them up in a park over in the heights somewhere.

One thing I learned from my dangling experience, besides not to tie myself fast ever again. That thing is strong. The lift is plenty powerful. It yanked me *up*. I don't need to be worried about the balloon having enough lift.

* * *

Next day, we helped launch and then chased them over into the wild mesa country north of the city. The balloon landed, very gently, not too far from a dirt road. We were standing around, when Jack said to me, "I hear you'd like a ride."

"Yes, Sir!" I said. "I sure would!"

"Hop in!"

It was almost too sudden. I was all interested in chasing, and still embarrassed about my little unplanned ride the day before. But there I was, in the basket. Jack pulled a string, and the propane burner roared, and we lifted off the ground, so gentle. He held onto the string, heating the air in the balloon more and more, and we went up and up. Pete and the others looked strange, from that angle. I was almost straight above them and going further up all the time. We drifted just a little toward the mountains.

Jack shut off the burner, and I couldn't believe how quiet it was. He leaned back and relaxed, but I was too excited. I could see the city, like a map, with all the streets and the freeways and the river and the tall buildings downtown and the green parks. We were over the brown brushy east mesa. The mountains were further east, still higher than we were. There wasn't a cloud in the sky.

Other balloons were up, too, some higher, some lower, some on one side and some on the other. I could sense the three dimensions of that space all the balloons were in. There's more room up there than it seems from the ground.

I felt something, probably what Pete calls the magic. Grandpap *would* like it, if he could get over his fear. It's so quiet. So peaceful, somehow. It's not a good way to travel from one place to another, maybe. But it's a good place to be, for a while, every once in a while.

I was thinking things like that when we landed. The basket bounced a couple of times, and almost tipped over. After we let the air out of the balloon, and stretched it out over the sage brush, Jack pulled out a bottle of champagne and started to push the cork out. Suddenly he handed it to me and said, "Pop it, and try to land the cork in the basket, for good luck."

"Me?"

"Sure. You're the new initiate. Push there."

I never had a champagne bottle in my hand before in my life. I could hardly move the plastic cork, but finally it slipped a little, and then suddenly it popped out and flew 'way up in the air. Actually, it came down near the basket, but didn't land in it. Maybe I'll have bad luck, but it didn't feel that way at the time.

Jack made me kneel and said some things to the other guys standing around, and poured some of the champagne on my head. I wasn't paying much attention to what he was saying. I was still floating in the peace and quiet up there, feeling good, wishing I could share this with Grandpap. The peace would do him good.

* * *

LOYALTY EROSION

Some day I'll hafta get ear plugs, thought Gibb, after a long, hard noise-filled day. The window beside his bed was fifty feet from the main north-south highway and traffic roared by at midnight. A body tries to drown it out with music on a clock radio, but even the FM stations talk and holler nowadays, trying to sell stuff nobody wants.

Gibb lay in bed, on a late Friday evening, enjoying stretching out straight at last. He felt his wife's cool smooth bottom against his leg and let himself relax. He heard the swish and shush of car tires on the road. When the motors were quiet, the noise was not unlike surf, but some motors in this part of the ghetto were extremely noisy, drilling right into a body's head and decomposing thoughts and memories. A siren sounded faintly, probably on the other side of the river.

If only we could get it quiet, he thought. The noises do bad things to me. We go to sleep with noise and wake up with noise. The traffic between here and school -- the bridge, the railroad tracks, the freeway -- it's all noise. The boys at school are noisy, especially when they're all yelling at the same time. At home it's the TV, and the stereo and the radio, upstairs and down. Earplugs might help.

We'll have a rest now for the next two days. Gibb rolled over and put his arm around Teresa. Lucky she's here in bed with me. She sure loves her big yellow-haired gringo.

He dreamed. He was looking out over the battlement of a

castle, defending against a medieval siege. He stood above a big wooden door shaped like a huge ear. Attackers came up and banged on the door with the hilts of their swords. He dumped a huge black kettle of hot oil down on them. Some of them screamed and the ear-door rattled more than ever. He had no more oil. He watched helplessly from the wall, while more attackers brought a huge log and began ramming the door with it. *Bang! Bang!* They'll break the door with that ramrod! *Bang! Bang!* Teresa yelled, "Who's there?"

Gibb felt her pull away from him and get up. *Bang! Bang!* The door will break soon.

"It's Mike!" He'll smash that door down. Take it easy, Mike, before you break the door.

"They're arresting Ricardo!" Mike always shouts. He doesn't talk -- he yells, too fast to understand, and so loud a body's inner ear rattles. What say, Mike? Quit hollering!

"They're arresting Ricardo!"

"Who is?"

"Some guy said he was a cop!"

"Why?"

"I don't know! But, come on, we can stop him, *maybe!*"

Gibb had one last thought of boiling oil, and then began pulling on his pants. He was stiff and had trouble tying his shoes. Teresa was big-eyed, and kept saying, "Oh, my God," and "Be careful," and things like that. She was already very scared. Gibb was mostly stiff and sleepy.

"Where is all this?"

"Right around the corner, between here and my place. Come on!" Mike was still yelling, and Gibb's ears were buzzing.

The two of them climbed into Mike's VW bus. "O.K., Mike. What the hell is going on?"

"I don't know! Me and Ricardo were working on an engine, over at my place. We finished and decided to go late to that party at Prof Smathers. Ricardo was on his way to your place in his car to clean up. I wash up and then come in my car. I get to this corner -- it's just up there -- and there's Ricardo

Loyalty Erosion   53

stopped, and another car's there, too. A guy has a gun on Ricardo -- he's standing with his hands on the roof of his car."
    Mike doesn't tell a story -- he yells. "I stop and ask what's the matter. Ricardo hollers, 'They're arresting me!'"
    Mike is spitting his story. "I ask what for, and the guy with the gun yells, 'Get the hell out of here, or I'll arrest you, too!' So I come for help."
    Gibb felt tired, and the VW bus engine was very noisy. Mike does have to yell, or I won't hear him, he thought. They turned off the boulevard onto a side street. Time to be in bed. Bed's a good place to be in the night.
    They could see a red light flashing almost like a red noise in the black silence. Silence -- red -- silence -- red. The red became bigger, louder, as they pulled nearer. Right in the middle of another dangerous intersecton, they pulled up and joined the gathering. Ricardo's VW bug was there, and another car, and a police car, with that blinking red light on top. From that same car a very bright spotlight shone directly into Gibb's face as he walked across the Y-shaped intersection.
    God, that light's loud, he thought. Hurts my face. Why are they shining it at me?
    A small man in a black uniform stood in the middle of the intersection. Gibb approached him. From the rear seat of the police car Gibb heard Ricardo call, "Mr. Jones!" He never could get over the habit of calling me that, since I was his teacher in school, not even after I married his mother.
    Gibb called, "Ricardo," and then spoke to the man in the black uniform. "What's he done?"
    "Failed to attend driving school." Gibb woke up more than he had so far since throwing the oil. It must be damn near midnight on Friday night. We're in the back streets of the South Valley. It's dark, and it's almost quiet.
    "What's he done tonight?"
    "He failed to attend driving school, and there's a warrant out for his arrest, and he's arrested!" Both face and voice sneered and insulted.

Gibb walked over to Ricardo. He was locked in the back seat of the police car, which was really a cage, with bars and wires. Ricardo was in pain, handcuffed and cramped, unable to really sit, with his arms twisted and locked behind him. Failed to attend driving school. Ricardo had been crying, or was on the verge of crying, with the combination of pain and anger. "What's going on?" Gibb asked.

"I don't know! Get the name of that one." He tossed his head toward the man in uniform.

I'll get names all right, but what the hell is this all about? Gibb went back to the policeman. "What is your name?"

"Officer Sowin."

"You're state police?"

"No, County Sheriff's Department."

"What happened here tonight?"

A man who had been standing next to the third car spoke up. "I stopped him."

"Why?"

"Reckless driving, driving on private land." Oh-oh. That dirt road cut-off near Mike's which avoids the traffic light on Bridge Boulevard.

"What's your name?"

"Blundy." His mild Texas accent makes me nervous and hostile, thought Gibb. He was dressed in slacks, open shirt, zipper jacket.

"Why are you stopping people?"

"County detective." Detective. *How* does he stop people? Blundy had short hair, pointed nose, thin mouth. His face looked tanned, but across his eyes was a pale stripe, probably from wearing sunglasses all day.

"What's this about driving school?" Gibb was fighting to keep calm, but his voice was rising a little.

"When I stopped him, I radioed in, and there's been a warrant out for his arrest since last September."

Gibb walked back to Ricardo. Mike was talking through the window. What a pair, and what a mess. Hard-working teenagers -- Mike, the loud one, with yellow hair, blue eyes, typical northern type -- Finland or some place. And Ricardo, his friend, small, dark, spunky, kinky hair -- looks afro in his little VW in the middle of the night. Teresa's boy, locked in a cage by these cocky bastards for no reason that they can explain. What the hell is really going on here?

A noisy wrecker drove up with a flashing blue light. Living color now. The flashing red light, the pale orange/brown street light, the bright white spot light, and now a blue flasher. A young man walked up to Blundy and they spoke. Gibb went over to them. "What's he after?"

"He came for this car." Blundy shrugged an elbow at Ricardo's little grey VW bug. The poor kid has to take it apart about every other week. He's learned a lot about motors, but it's a never-ending job, trying to keep it running without spending more money on it than he has.

"What's wrong with the car?"

"Nothing's wrong with it." Blundy seemed to think he shouldn't have to bother with all these questions. Is his voice also rising just a little bit? "But I'm responsible for it. I'm not leaving it here all night to be stolen. And *he* can't take care of it, 'cause he's going to *jail!*" He nodded toward the police car cage.

"And where's he think he's taking it?" Gibb asked.

"To city hall, I guess. I don't really care where he takes it."

"Why the rush? Why didn't you call me to take it home?"

"We didn't know you were coming. We had no idea *you* existed."

"I bet you didn't!" Gibb's voice squealed a little. Stop a kid you think is black, find he's brown, and accidentally stir up a goddam Viking! You sure as hell had no idea I was coming! Well, I'm here, and I'll get to the bottom of this shit.

Blundy smiled, if that's the word for it. More like a grimace, or maybe a gas pain. "Well, if you want to settle with him," shrugging toward the wrecker driver, "that's O.K. with me, but I'm not going to be responsible for leaving that car here."

Gibb looked at the wrecker driver, who was plainly embarrassed. "I pay you to go away?"

"Well, the boss really raises hell if I go out in the middle of the night and don't bring anything back."

"I'm driving that car home," Gibb stated flatly.

"Look, I'll split the fee with you. It's usually seven-fifty. Settle for three-seventy-five." My, he came up with that idea in a hurry. He just wants to get the hell outa here. I wonder who he splits it with usually.

Gibb didn't have his wallet. Driving without a license! No, Mike was driving. Gibb went over to Mike and Ricardo. Mike had three dollars. Ricardo said he had a dollar loose in his pants pocket. Gibb asked if he could get into Ricardo's pocket for that dollar. The policeman unlocked the back door of the car. Ricardo leaned over, and Gibb reached into his pocket and felt around among comb and keys and coins until he felt the dirty paper dollar. "I'll be driving the car home, too," Gibb said, and kept the keys.

"O.K." Ricardo was sounding weary.

Mike paid the wrecker and it roared away. Gibb asked Sowin about warrants. "How can a warrant get to be eight months old? The boy lives at home. He could have been arrested by telephone at any time in the last eight months."

Sowin didn't know. He didn't think Ricardo needed to be informed of it at the time the judge signed it.

"You just keep 'em by the radio?" Gibb asked.

The policeman squinted. These guys all have gas pains. Gibb asked what they were waiting for.

"City cops. The warrant was filed by and for the city."

"Oh, but you county guys use 'em to pick up people, too."

"We just stop 'em. Now the city has to come get him."

Gibb waited with Mike and Ricardo, while all three of them became more and more angry. At last another flashing red light appeared. A shiny blue city police car pulled up and two laughing, red-cheeked young cops got out. They joked with Sowin, saying they had been delayed because they were raiding a whore house. They kidded about the girls, and the owner whom they all seemed to know, but Gibb didn't really listen. His head throbbed. Sowin let Ricardo out of the cage. A city cop put a second pair of handcuffs on him. Sowin unlocked, with great difficulty and delay, the first pair of handcuffs. Gibb asked where they were going. One of the city cops said, "City jail. You can come and get him for fifty dollars bail. Cash." The city cops locked Ricardo in their back seat cage and drove away. The white police car drove away. Blundy drove away in his unmarked car.

Gibb breathed a sigh of relief when Ricardo's little car started. Half the time it doesn't, he muttered to himself. He drove it home, four blocks, not believing that what had happened had happened. Mike followed in his VW bus.

Gibb and Mike found Teresa frantic with worry. They told her what seemed to be happening. "Fifty dollars! We don't have that much cash, and they won't take a check. How do we get cash in the middle of the night? He'll be there all week-end!"

Gibb heard a siren, probably across the river. "Sons of bitches!" he bellowed.

Teresa cried out, "No! We *do* have fifty dollars. That down payment Mrs. Barr gave me for material for a suit I'm making for her. We'll use that."

They all piled into Mike's noisy bus. While he drove, he explained in shouts what he had figured out about the warrant. "Remember that ticket Ricardo got last April for a hundred dollars? Just a year ago, it was! Accused him of going sixty-five in a thirty-five-mile zone, from a dead stop a hundred feet back. Judge threw the ticket out and told the cop he oughta have more goddam sense. Then he added, to Ricardo, like an after-thought, because he looks so young, 'You attend driving school.' Ricardo was so relieved about the hundred dollars that he didn't object."

Gibb remembered some of it. Ricardo didn't tell his family as much as he told outsiders, but Mike would know that kind of thing.

Mike continued. "Well, he was supposed to go to driving school in June, but the first day he was to report was the day of that riot, remember? when that gang of students broke all the store windows on Central? Ricardo went to city hall to attend driving school, and no one was there but a scared and nasty secretary. She told him to get the hell out of there, so he did, and he never went back."

"So," Gibb said, "the damn judge signed a bench warrant, or some flunky stamped it, last September, and no one ever told Ricardo. They just keep 'em by the radio, and jerks like Blundy stop all and sundry, especially if they look young and black." Gibb's voice was shrill over the noise of the microbus. "By God, I intend to raise one helluva lot of hell," he growled in quieter fury.

Teresa looked at him with her big brown eyes, scared. "Let's get him out of there first."

"Yeah, O.K. But I'm going to raise hell."

The bus rattled to a stop in the parking lot in front of the new city hall. Bluish lights glared, bouncing off marble and concrete. They found the city desk, all marble and mahogany and white lights, with footfalls reverberating outward into empty halls and rooms. A couple of twenty-year-old girls stood around, refusing to look up into anyone's face. A skinny, big-nosed middle-aged man smoked cigarettes and paced in front of the desk. He must have had metal taps on his heels, the way every footstep clanged on the marble floor.

The desk was like a booth at a fair, with two men trapped inside a four-sided counter. It looked like they were in jail. Gibb wondered how they got in there. One was in a blue uniform and the other in street clothes. Mike and Teresa talked with them. Gibb said nothing, but studied both men carefully. The plainclothesman seemed to be higher in rank, but he was much more stupid and insensitive. He kept waving the questions over to the uniformed city policeman.

Gibb paid the bail with the money Teresa had pressed on him

while they were coming in the car. He had to sign something. It looked strange -- blue paper and fine black print, with the typed words, "failure to attend driving school," the typed name, "Ricardo Sanchez," and a scrawl across one line, "Gibb Jones." Not a name they expected, I bet.

Then nothing happened for a very long time. What's taking so long? "Well, they have to book him before they can release him. It takes a while." The uniformed man smiled and spoke softly and courteously.

Gibb asked him, "What's the process for filing a formal complaint?"

"What do you want to complain about?"

"I want to complain about Blundy, cruising the back streets of the South Valley, scaring people, pulling guns on them, stopping them, frisking them, searching their cars, radioing headquarters and finding eight-month-old warrants on file, handcuffing and abusing people, confiscating their automobiles, and insulting other concerned people who object." Gibb was awake, thinking as clearly as he did in the daytime.

The policeman never lost the courtesy and seeming sensitivity, but he was no help at all, and Gibb felt his ears becoming warm. "You'll have to make that complaint at the County Sheriff Department."

Ricardo came through a doorway with a young uniformed policeman. He looked sheepish. His loose loafers scuffed on the marble floor. His fuzzy hair stood out from his head, reminding Gibb of a picture of a koala bear he had once seen. He was rubbing his wrists. "Can we go now?" he asked.

The police escort handed some papers to the one inside the cage/desk. "O.K. See you on Tuesday at eleven, in court."

"Yeah, if you say so," murmured Ricardo.

Gibb had no interest in the jokes between Ricardo and Mike, as the two of them skipped down the marble steps outside. He stopped on the top step. Teresa asked what was the matter. Gibb could hear cars moving on pavement, far away, but it was quiet and still right there where they were. Gibb asked,

"Where's the County Sheriff Department?"

"Over there," answered Mike, pointing to an old concrete building two empty parking lots away.

"I'm going over there," Gibb said.

"We'll all go," agreed Teresa. Anger was rising in her voice, now that Ricardo was out and she could let go of fear.

They found an unlocked plate glass door. Gibb noticed that it was one in the morning. An old man with a pointed nose and whiskers like a mouse sat behind a high counter with an old telephone switchboard behind him. He had never heard of Blundy. Gibb began to suspect that Blundy was some kind of private vigilante. The mouse at the desk did know of Sowin. "Yes, he's on duty at this time." It was very quiet in the empty room.

Gibb asked about the process of filing formal complaints. Mouse had no idea, but in less than a minute five other policemen, all in uniform, came through a door behind the switchboard. None of them knew of any process for filing formal complaints. Gibb wondered if they understood him, or if it was a pretended language barrier. They spoke in Spanish to each other, but when Gibb switched to Spanish, they became even more stupid-sounding. *"¿Queja?* -- complaint? No, you can't."

One of them thought Santos Baca would know. "Where's he?" Gibb asked. "I'll call him immediately."

"You can't."

"Why not?"

"He's on vacation. Come back Monday."

The buzzing in Gibb's head became disturbing again. "I need to file a complaint tonight. Blundy isn't on vacation. He's out harrassing people right now!"

None of the six could answer. Finally the one who spoke in the name of Santos Baca said, "We don't know and we don't care. Get out of here. You have no business here. You are creating a disturbance."

Disturbance! Gibb spoke very softly. "I was sleeping, minding my own business, when this started. Blundy created the disturbance." The figures behind the counter became cartoon-like -- Mouse and two Guinea Pigs, Hamster, and Speaker Mole, the one with the thick glasses. "Let's get out of here," Gibb murmured to his companions.

They crossed the parking lots in a dark quiet daze. The rattle of the VW motor did not disturb their thoughts. Those damn Texans are loose on the streets, picking on blacks and browns, and you come here to bitch and find these stupid Uncle Toms covering for them. Your local police are armed and dangerous. Support your local Gestapo. I need a bumper sticker like that. Get me twenty tickets a day.

Gibb lay in bed with an arm around Teresa. There was less traffic out on the street, fifty feet from his ear. It wasn't quite constant, but he heard every car approach, from half a mile away in either direction.

He comes home from school, and in the door. Teresa usually calls, "Hi-hi," but not this time. He opens the bedroom door and finds a cop in black uniform on top of Teresa on the bed. She's yelling, but not making any sound. Gibb grabs the pistol from the cop's holster and clubs the back of his head with it. He rolls off onto the floor and Gibb shoots three times, completely demolishing the entire cloacal region of the cop.

He sat up in bed. Jesus, I'm not even dreaming. I'm lying here in bed wide awake with my eyes open thinking shit like that. What is happening to me?

"Lie down close to me," Teresa whispered. He lay down again. He recalled a conversation he and Ricardo had once, about catching a prowler in the house. Instead of turning him over to the police, they tie his hands behind him and leave him hanging from a rafter by the wrists for a couple of days. We need to do that to Blundy.

Gibb shook himself all over in a full-length shudder. They're messing up my head! I'm just like them! Or they're real live embodiments of the worst of me. Good God!

The family went through the week-end in a dazed stupor. Teresa worked in the sewing room, and Gibb refinished a couple of chairs. On Monday Gibb told his classes at school what had happened. The students picked up on his fury, and told stories of their own. Two of the teachers told him to write it, for the school paper. He was more inclined to save it for some kind of formal complaint, maybe even a lawsuit.

Gibb and Teresa drove back to the County Sheriff Department on Monday after school. "If that Blundy ever tries to stop me..." Gibb muttered.

"He won't," Teresa snapped, "'cause you're not black."

A strikingly good-looking dark-haired girl greeted them at the rodent desk, but she too had never hear of Blundy. How about Santos Baca? That can't be the right name, Gibb thought. The grammar's fractured, but that means "holy cow."

"You're looking for the defective division," she said.

"I know."

"The *detective* division."

"Yes. Where's that?"

"Down the hall there, through that glass door, all the way to the end of the big room, through a door to the left, downstairs and through the first door on your right."

Gibb didn't say thanks. Courtesy was worn too thin. He and Teresa followed those directions, and the door to the right led them smack out of the building into a very busy parking lot. Gibb was so angry he became unreasonable. He marched Teresa all around the building, in another door obviously marked, "County Treasurer," and asked for the detective division. The elderly lady never batted an eye. "Down those stairs and that's it."

They went down a dark, dirty, unswept, unlit, unpainted stairway, and came to two desks with girls behind each, and two dirty stuffed chairs. Gibb marched straight to the first desk. "We're looking for Santos Baca."

"He's on vacation."

"When will he return?"

"May tenth."

Gibb stopped. It was April 30. "Who is his immediate

superior?"

She hesitated. "That would be the sheriff."

"Where is he?"

"His office is upstairs, but he's never there. He's always sick."

"What is the procedure for registering a formal complaint?"

"What sort of complaint?"

"A complaint, and maybe a suit, against a certain Blundy, who says he works for this department."

"Just a moment." She walked down the dark, dirty, paper-littered hall.

Gibb noticed how her behind swayed from side to side, and thought, "She'll fall off those high-heeled shoes."

She wobbled back. "If you'll wait here just a few minutes, Sergeant Baker will talk to you."

"Very well." Gibb felt his anger, but wasn't sure the bureau noticed or cared. His courtesy was a mockery of real human consideration. What kind of people do they get to work in a dump like this? he wondered to himself.

He had no intention of sitting in either filthy chair, but Teresa squatted gingerly on the edge of one and motioned to Gibb with a downward patting of the palm of her hand to do the same. "Take it easy," she murmured. Yes, I'd better, or we'll get Ricardo into worse trouble in court tomorrow morning.

Some time passed and then a young black in blue uniform approached. He was as good-looking as Sidney Poitier, only shorter. He did not walk past, as Gibb expected, but went directly to Gibb and announced, "I'm Sergeant Baker."

"I'm Gibb Jones and this is my wife."

"Come back into my office where we can talk."

"Yes, we'd better." They went to a very small square room. The large desk nearly filled it with two straight chairs on one side and one on the other. Filing cabinets were in three of the four corners. Sergeant Baker closed the door and sat down. The sergeant's jacket, and a shoulder holster with pistol, hung on a hook on the back of the door. Gibb and Teresa sat stiffly on the edges of their chairs.

"I understand you want to ask about the case of Ricardo Sanchez," Baker said, opening a folder and leafing past yellow papers to get at a blue one.

How does he know that? Gibb wondered. I asked about Blundy. I never mentioned Ricardo's name. This guy already knew what we wanted before he asked our names just now in the hall. They *do* communicate in here. That stupidity is a sham, a cover-up for something else. "Does a man named Blundy work for this department?"

"Yes."

"What is his position?"

"He's a detective."

"Exactly what is he authorized to do?"

"What is the purpose of these questions?"

"I have to decide whether to sue Blundy or the outfit Blundy works for, if any. I need information."

"What do you want to sue for?"

Gibb hesitated. "I'm wondering about keeping warrants..."

Baker interrupted him. "Did you read the warrant?"

"Yes."

"What did it say?"

"It said, 'Failure to attend driving school'."

Baker rose and reached in a filing cabinet and pulled out another blue paper. "No, I don't mean that part. If you're objecting to the reason for the warrant, you're in the wrong department. You'll have to see the judge about that. Did you read the rest of the warrant?"

"You mean all that fine print? No."

"Well, you should read it. It *commands* three agencies -- city, county and state police -- to bring the person named to the judge. I don't question the reason stated on the line you read. When I get a warrant, I serve it."

"You *didn't* serve it, since last September! You could have arrested Ricardo by telephone! Or was that warrant just filled out last Friday night?"

"Do you believe that?"
"I strongly suspect it."
Baker slammed the filing cabinet shut. "Well, if you believe that, what's the use of our talking?"
Gibb never moved. "Tell us about the right of a plain-clothes detective to search someone."
Baker became a teacher, or a reciting student. "Search is legal in three cases." He counted. Index finger -- "Search with permission of the suspect." Middle finger -- "Search with a warrant." Ring finger -- "Search attendant to arrest."
Gibb felt his voice getting squeaky again. "So, once Blundy started searching Ricardo, he *had* to arrest him, and if he arrests him, that makes the search legal! He certainly had no warrant and no permission."
"What do you object to? There *was* a warrant! He stopped the right person."
"Failure to attend driving school."
"You have to take *that* complaint to the judge."
"I object to Blundy stopping people for no reason in the middle of the night, scaring them out of their wits --"
Baker interrupted again. "How do you know he scared him?"
Teresa exploded, for the first time. "He said so! It would scare anybody to be stopped in the middle of the night at gunpoint and be searched and handcuffed."
"Handcuffs are part of the procedure for any arrest. That won't hold up in court."
"What won't?" Gibb asked.
"That one person tells another he's scared. He'll have to give his own testimony. Why are you here, anyway? I really don't think you want anything except to give me a hard time. *You* weren't arrested. Ricardo is an adult, and he'll have to look out for himself."
Teresa spoke softly. "He's my son, and we care plenty what happens to him."
"What is he to him?" Baker asked Teresa, pointing at Gibb.
"As sovereign citizen, I object --"

Baker interrupted once more. "Listen. You don't need to come in here and yell at me. You need to get yourself a lawyer who will explain to you the law!"

Gibb and Teresa looked at each other. "What about police in unmarked cars making arrests?" Gibb asked.

Baker laughed. "You gotta be kidding me!"

Gibb's vision clouded a little. This damned black man does the white man's dirty work better than any white man could. Worse than the rodent desk in the middle of the night. No, you black bastard, I'm not kidding. How much of that did I say out loud? Not much, maybe -- he's still laughing.

"Why, the FBI make arrests, and they're not uniformed or in marked cars."

"Do they?"

"Oh, come on! How long you been in this country?"

"Too long," Gibb murmured. He recalled SNCC workers in Atlanta years before, who fully expected that Daddy Ho and Daddy Mao would come and rescue them. Poor bastards, no wonder they were so crazy.

"What do you think the FBI does?" Baker asked with a sneer.

"I've seen them kill people, but that was on TV. I thought they made investigations."

"And what do they do with those investigations?"

"Turn them over to the local police."

"Oh," Baker grinned, leaning way back in his chair so that the front legs came off the floor. "They haven't worked that way for years."

Gibb looked at the whites of Baker's eyes. "You tell Blundy that if he tries to stop *me* in the black dark night in the back streets of the South Valley in an unmarked car, I'm not stopping. I'll run over him!"

Baker leaped to the door, banging the pistol against it, reached into one of the pockets of the jacket and pulled out a black wallet. He flipped it open and displayed a yellow badge on one panel and a card under a plastic window on the other. He yelled, "When I'm stopping someone, I show him this, and if I show you this, and you don't stop, I'll stop you." He pointed with his index finger, like a boy playing cops and robbers.

Gibb sneered, unblinking. "And how do I know that you haven't just escaped from a mental hospital and stolen that at the five-and-dime?"

Baker didn't notice Gibb's cleverness, or courage. "If I show you this, and you don't stop --" His eyes were popping, with the whites showing all around, "I'll stop you!"

Teresa pulled on Gibb's arm. "We better get out of here. He doesn't understand us at all." Gibb saw her fear for Ricardo. They didn't say any goodbyes. They found their way out of the building not really seeing anything, feeling their way through dark, mouldy, stale-smelling cellar corridors. "I'll stop you!" echoed in their thoughts.

They can stop me, or anybody, Gibb thought. The Bill of Attainder is back in effect. Stop all and sundry, at any time.

The next morning Ricardo was arraigned. It took thirty seconds. The judge said, "This case is closed, when you attend driving school." He waved his hand and refused to listen to attempted explanations about riots last summer or inappropriately rough treatment over the previous weekend.

Gibb considered suing, but then figured some lawyer would take the money and do nothing. Baker's probably right. Ricardo himself checked with Legal Aid, but they weren't interested in initiating a suit -- they just help with "defense."

Gibb attempted to warn the general public. He wrote down an account of what happened, but when he showed it to people, they thought it was fiction. "This didn't really happen!"

He took his story to the local newspaper. An assistant editor read it all the way through, which was something. But when he looked up, his eyes were tired and bored. "Too long."

"It's not news?" squealed Gibb.

"Well, I hate to say this, but it's not really unusual. This kind of thing happens all the time."

Gibb felt excited about *that* admission. "Well, surely there's a story for you *there!* A reporter could interview me, and Ricardo!"

"Tell you what," said the weary editor. "Reduce this to seven hundred words and I'll run it as a letter. My normal limit on letters is five hundred, but I'll make an exception."

Gibb felt more tired than the editor. Not news. Just another crank letter and who reads them, besides other cranks? He wrote a letter, but he never saw it in the paper.

A public relations article from the police department appeared in the paper, requesting respect and co-operation from the general public. Gibb wrote a furious letter in reply, which they did print, in which he stated that the police would get respect and co-operation from him, maybe, after he received a bushel of abject apolgies from them first. He never saw any result from the letter.

Gibb lay beside Teresa in bed in the middle of the night. Twenty dogs from the kennel across the street were howling and barking. A motorcycle with no muffler roared by. There oughta be laws against such disturbance of the peace. Ha! There are! Call the cops. Ha!

Gibb heard sirens across the river. The dogs were going crazy. The sirens approached, crossing the bridge. Call the cops, and get insulted some more. Three cars with sirens blaring and screaming full blast roared by the house, going at least a hundred. Teresa jerked and opened her eyes. "What? What?"

"It's O.K.," Gibb murmured, cradling and cuddling her. She quieted immediately and fell back asleep. But it isn't O.K., he thought. We'll survive this, somehow, but we'll have to do it alone. The public thing is destroyed. Now it's part of the problem, part of the enemy we must outsmart and outlive. What's left is all private, all on the inside. At last he slept.

* * *

DUKE CITY ALCHEMIST

Chapter One

I'm worried about Dad. And there doesn't seem to be any normal channel to take my worries to -- I mean, there may not be a thing the matter. Probably there isn't. We live here together peacefully enough. Mama died just before I divorced Epifanio. I think maybe I waited for her to be gone, so she'd miss all the trauma and legal mess.

It was Dad's idea that I move in here with him on Isidro Boulevard. Not really a nice section of town -- too much traffic and noise to be "just right" -- but a cute little adobe house that's very comfortable, and near my work downtown.

Dad was alone and wanted the company. And I needed to start my life over in a new place. My kids are grown and gone, and I didn't need old reminders of all that alcoholic marriage misery to haunt me -- so I was ready.

Dad and Mama lived here together for ten years after they married. He isn't really my father. Mama raised me without a father. I was so glad when she found Dad -- someone who'd be good to her, and treat her right, and make her feel good about herself.

By that time, it was continual put-downs for me from Epifanio. Beatings, even. I suppose it's fair to say that if it wasn't for Dad, I'd hate all men and be done with it. He's different, somehow -- doesn't have that macho thing.

He encouraged me to go to the U. after I moved in with him. "Go! Learn everything! Don't worry about their worthless degrees. Enjoy finding out things. Look for connections." It was excellent advice. I finally majored in philosophy and minored in Spanish literature. Talk about worthless degrees...

But now I'm worried about Dad. His health seems all right, except he's restless at night. I wake up at three in the morning and notice his light on and find him sitting at his desk reading, or writing. Or I get up to go to the bathroom, and there he is, sitting in the dark in the middle of the living room, cross-legged like a yogi with his hands cupped upward in his lap, unmoving. Meditating, or in trance.

I ask him next morning what he's doing, and he says, "Taking Mind Games a step further."

I suggest he needs more sleep and he says, "What for? I'm fine. I'm *busy!*"

I suggest a physical check-up and he gets angry. "What for? I can tell more about how I feel and how my body works than they can. And I'm not predisposed to find something *wrong* and then take pay for making it worse, the way they are."

When I asked to see his medical insurance policy, he stunned me, growling, "I don't have one. That's just asking for trouble in advance."

I'm not sure how old he is. His stamina and his behavior seem appropriate for men younger than he is. I mean he acts and looks younger than I know he has to be. He doesn't talk much about his life before he came here and married Mama. Came from "back East." This is still the Old West -- we don't care what you did, or what you're running away from. Here it's a fresh start. What can you do? What kind of person are you?

I found this job as a reporter for the newspaper. The boss liked my stuff from the start. Maybe the female angle helped, and the chicana angle besides. Sure didn't hurt any, which means that times have changed -- a little. Now I write a column several times a week. HUNK O' LOGIC.

So the old philosophy degree pays off. Logic is not so worthless after all. There's a lot going on in the world that isn't logical, let me say. I dig up stuff, mostly local, and write it all out. Stirs up quite a bit of interest in the paper, which the boss likes.

Dad has led me to some of my stories. I'll never forget one -- in fact it was the first time I became conscious that I was

Chapter One

worrying about him. He was on the phone when I came in.

"I need to speak to the person who made the decision to close the dump on Mondays."

There were pauses -- I only heard his end of it. "Surely the person who made that decision doesn't answer the phone... Yes, I'll hold... I'm calling to find out the reasons why the dump is closed on Mondays... The day sacred to the moon -- Tuesdays, too? The day sacred to an obscure Scandinavian war god?" Dad can combine anger and sarcasm.

"I have my pick-up loaded to the goddam sky, tied on with rope -- and I've already driven to the dump and back, and now I find that I, sovereign citizen and supposed technical *owner* of the dump, do not own a dump after all, until forty-eight hours from now. In the meantime I have to haul this half-ton of *crap* all over town, wherever I go for the next two days."

He shook his head as he listened. "I don't sense any of that, Sir. Why was I not informed of this very bizarre decision? I mean, what's wrong with Monday and Tuesday?... I missed it... I see... You're trying to arouse the citizenry about your slashed budget. Well, it worked in one case!"

He spluttered and protested further. I couldn't suppress a giggle, and he looked up and saw me. I went to him and touched his shoulder. He took my hand, and had to grin. Then he winked. I decided that some of his fury was a pose, that time. And yet he was white with rage at the beginning of the phone call. I made a good column out of it.

So why am I worried? He's a cantankerous, eccentric, remarkably healthy, headstrong old man. What's wrong with that?

Well, I've been hesitating to put this down, I think, but here goes. Sometimes I can't find him.

That looks stupid, now that I have it written. Sometimes you can't find him, eh, Marta? Well, big deal. You haven't looked very well. You just missed him. He turned up, didn't he?

Yes, but I can't find him sometimes, and I panic. I called Clyde next door once, but Dad wasn't over there. Clyde's afraid of him, I've decided, and I know Dad doesn't respect Clyde much at all. Certainly not enough for Dad to bother going over there and staying very long.

Just this morning I call Dad to lunch. It's a little early, but I have an appointment for 12:30, and I'm thinking we'll have lunch over with before I leave. "Dad?" No answer.

Not in his bedroom/study.

Not in his woodworking shop downstairs.

I go outside. His pick-up's where it should be. He's not in the garage. Not in the worm beds. Not at the woodpile. Not at his compost bins. Not at the rabbit hutches. Nowhere in the garden. I look through the fence over into Clyde's yard. No sign of him. Clyde's out of town anyway until tomorrow.

I go out front and stare up and down the street. No sign of him. I even walk to the little meat market and ask, "You folks seen Dad?"

"Nope. He hasn't been here for several days."

I go back and pick up the phone. I'm not sure just what I had in mind -- missing persons, maybe. It's happened before, and I'm afraid his absent-mindedness is going to turn into a real problem. I glance up and he's standing in his study, looking at me!

"Lunch ready?" he asks.

"Where have you been?" I yell.

"Been? Right here. Why?"

"I been looking all over for you! Didn't you hear me call?"

"I thought maybe I heard something. I was -- concentrating."

"Where were you?"

"Sittin' right here."

"You were not! I came in here first, looking."

"Maybe I was in the bathroom just then."

"No, you weren't --" But I'm not absolutely certain. I thought I was, but I'm not. Maybe I should worry more about myself. Maybe I have the problem. Feels silly now. I wonder if it helps to write down this vague indefinite worry.

* * *

Dad and I go to Mind Games once a week. It's a group, meets in a church. "Never thought they'd get me in a church again," Dad growled the first time the group met. But he loves

Chapter One

it. Too much, maybe, I sometimes think.

Some years ago, psychologists were doing experiments with dope, LSD especially. Then the government got into it with that strange notion of "illegal substances." Instead of quitting the experiments, the doctors found they could induce the same kind of "tripping out," if I may call it that, by guided trances. They called it all MIND GAMES, and wrote a book.

A group of us began working our way through the exercises in the book, meeting once a week. We take turns being Leader. Everyone else stretches out on the floor and participates in a Mind Game.

I go to the Magic Theater and see a full-length performance of CRIME AND PUNISHMENT, in ten minutes. Time perception is changed. Dad was Leader that night.

Another time we're supposed to go back and re-live a happy experience from childhood. I'm a little dubious. My childhood wasn't what you'd call happy. I'm happier now, working at an interesting job and feeling good about myself and living peacefully here with Dad.

Anyway, I go into the trance, down the long staircase to that other state of mind, and I re-live a horrible experience. It's a fight with a childhood chum, supposedly my best friend. I'd forgotten it -- repressed it immediately after it happened, no doubt. But in Mind Games, I remembered how she teased me about having no father, and how I raged at her for thinking her worthless drunken bum of an old man was something better than what I had, which was no father at all!

I come out of the game in a rage, white and trembling. If she'd been in the room, I would have killed her. I haven't seen her in twenty years. But all that fury was bottled up in me all that time -- I'm shaking now, remembering it.

So that's Mind Games. We stare into each other's eyes, and see strange ancient faces. Dad says he communicated with a potted plant once. Others in the group suspect him of making up his reactions, but I don't think he'd do that.

Coming home tonight, I ask him about the game. I was Leader. They were supposed to have an extra-terrestrial experience. During the game I saw Dad raise his arms and cup his hands, as if holding a huge ball. He was moving it around in front of his chest slowly.

"What was your extra-terrestrial journey?" I ask him. He didn't share with the group this time.

"I talked to Sol."

"Who's Saul?" I ask. I figure some Jewish friend from his past back East.

"No, Sol. S-O-L. The Sun."

"You communicated with the Sun," I repeat.

"The Sun is a sentient being," Dad intones. It sounds like a quotation.

"Oh. That was the game, eh? Talking with the Sun." He's silent. "What did he say?" I ask.

"He said I had answered the first question." Dad's very serious, almost in a trance state again. He's staring ahead out the windshield without seeing anything.

"What's the first question?" I ask.

"What do you want?"

"Nothing particular. Just trying to find out about your Mind Game tonight," I say.

"No. That's the first question," he says with infinite patience.

"What is?"

"What do you want?"

"Oh." We're silent. Dad talks to the Sun, and he -- the Sun, a sentient being -- tells him that he's answered the first question. "What *do* you want, Dad?" I ask quietly, feeling the old worry thing again.

"Peace and quiet." He lapses into deep silence -- I can feel it somehow, so I don't say any more.

Our place here on Isidro Boulevard *is* very noisy. Traffic, trucks, motorcycles, airplanes, chain saws, dogs barking. "Do a thing on Ninety-five Decibels!" Dad shouted at me once, as half a dozen motorcycles roared by out front, drowning our conversation. "A body can't meditate in all this noise!" He was still yelling, even after the roar was further away.

"A body can't even hear his own roof brain chatter! The interference -- rraagh!" He roared like a lion, as if he could

Chapter One

silence the sources, or move all the noise-makers away, by roaring himself.

So Dad wants peace and quiet. I did do a HUNK O' LOGIC thing on his Ninety-five Decibels. The county has a noise-control ordinance which fixes that as the maximum allowed. Ninety-five decibels. But the sheriff's department has no personnel to enforce it. And there wasn't much public reaction to my column, either, that I noticed.

* * *

I had another very upsetting experience looking for Dad. I think he's in his study and call to him -- would he like a cup of tea? No answer. I go to his door and the room's empty. I shrug my shoulders and go put the teakettle on -- he's taught me to like it. My childhood conditioned me to think of tea as medicine. The only time Mama ever made it was when one of us was sick. So when I first moved in, whenever Dad asked me if I wanted tea, I'd say, "No, thanks. I feel fine." We still kid about it.

Anyway, I walk past his open door to go to the bathroom, while the teapot warms up, and he's sitting at his desk! "Dad! How long have you been sitting there?" He snaps out of a kind of trance, and blinks his eyes and stares at me.

"I dunno," he says. "Why?"

"How long? I need to know!"

He pulls his watch from his pocket and looks at it. "Half an hour, I'd say. Why?"

"I looked in here, not ten minutes ago, and the room was empty. You weren't here!"

"Sure, I was."

"No --" I'm alarmed, but I realize I'm sounding silly.

"How 'bout a cup of tea?" he says, getting up. "I'm feelin' fine!" And he winks.

I'm shaken, and he seems to want to calm me down. He follows me into the kitchen, while I make the tea. "What's your latest HUNK O' LOGIC?" he asks. It's obvious that he's trying to change the subject, but I'm so upset I let him.

"The story of a woman who has opened a 'Jog-with-a-Doberman' business," I say.

"Jog-with-a-Doberman," he echoes.

"Male chauvinists are always bothering lone woman joggers. Rape has not yet been eradicated in Duke City, much less harrassment. So this woman has bought half a dozen trained Dobermans that she rents out as jogging companions. Says her customers are delighted. The men back off. It's logical."

"Too bad such a thing is needed," Dad mutters.

"It sure as hell is," I reply. I'm still upset.

"Do they have the dogs on leashes?" Dad asks.

"Who?"

"The joggers. That's the law, you know. A dog must be on its owner's place behind a fence that holds it in, or on a leash."

"I don't know -- I'll have to call and ask about that. Why?" I wonder aloud.

"Oh, just wondering." He has a kind of dreamy look in his eye again. His attention wanders off, that way, and this time it sets me off.

"Where do you go, Dad?" I cry, very upset.

"Go? When?"

"Your mind goes away. You go into -- into a goddam Mind Games trance, or something. You worry me!"

"You sound angry," he says calmly. "I'm not hurting anybody, am I?"

"You're making *me* worry about you! Are you all right?"

"I'm fine," he says, getting up. "Thanks for the tea," he adds and goes to his study.

Later Clyde comes over, through the gate between the gardens, and knocks gently on the kitchen door. "Mr. Myers home?" he asks timidly. Clyde is the original Caspar Milquetoast. I'm surprised he wants Dad.

"Hi, Neighbor. I think he's in his study."

"Oh." Clyde sounds disappointed.

"You wanta talk to him?"

"No."

"C'mon in. You look like you're afraid, or something. Why'd you ask about Dad?"

Chapter One

"Can you come out here? So we can talk?"

I go out in the back yard. I figure we'd sit a while under the flowering trumpet vines, but Clyde leads me to the compost bins. Dad spends a great deal of time there. From one bin to another, he shovels leaves, grass clippings, rabbit droppings, horse manure he hauls in, dog droppings he gathers from all the strays that visit our place, table scraps. Dad says he doesn't need to jog for exercise. He gets all he needs shoveling. "What is it, Clyde?" I ask.

"I'm getting really worried about Mr. Myers."

"Why?"

"Maybe he should be locked up."

"Locked up! Whatever for?"

"I'm afraid he may become a danger, to himself, if no one else."

"What are you talking about?" I cry, feeling more annoyed than worried. "You're being silly."

"Yesterday I watched him, through the grape vine fence there," Clyde says, pointing.

"You were spying on him?"

"I -- watched him," Clyde repeats. "Here he was, on his hands and knees, in front of this pile of -- of *shit!* With his nose an inch away from it. Staring, glaring, sniffing. I tell you, it was weird. I was afraid he was gonna start eating it!"

I have to laugh. "Let me tell you, that's one thing Dad won't do! Not figuratively, and certainly not literally. He even made up a word for it! Coprophagia!"

"Marta, I think you should be worried about him," Clyde insists. "I sure am. He's off his rocker. He always was strange, but now he's flipped out. You should get help, before something serious happens."

"Just because you saw him studying his beloved compost up close? Come now, Clyde. He's eccentric, but he's not dangerous."

"There's more. This morning he was out at the chicken coop, talking to the chickens! I heard him."

"And you eavesdropped on him."

"When a crazy man is talking crazy talk to the chickens,

you're not eavesdropping if you listen!" Clyde exclaims.

I suppress a laugh. We walk toward the chicken pens. I've been concerned about Dad, but Clyde's worries seem simply silly. Looking at compost. Talking to chickens. "So, what did he say?"

"'Can you hear it, Ladies?' he asked. They clucked back at him. He repeated it. 'Can you hear it?' He stuck his head down inside this nest box here and held it there a long time. Then he went around and knelt down and talked to them through the wire. 'I can hear it when I get close, there in your nest,' he says. 'I don't like it,' he says. 'Scares me. But it doesn't seem to bother you, does it, Ladies?' They whine back at him. 'You seem to like it. You're thriving on it. An egg apiece every day ever since.'"

"Ever since what?" I ask.

"How should I know?" wails Clyde. "I tell you, he's crazy."

"Like I say, eccentric. But hardly dangerous." We walk to the back patio and sit. The perfume of four o'clocks is almost overpowering. "I don't know why you're so concerned."

"I worry about you, Marta," Clyde says.

"Me? Believe me, Dad's no danger to me. We get along fine."

Clyde wishes I'd be interested in him. He thinks I'm his girl friend, or something. I don't mind being friendly, but I can't take Clyde seriously. He's such a sissy, such a scairdy-cat, such a fussy -- oh, I don't know. I think of him as a friendly neighbor, but he wants it to be a lot more than that.

"I thought he was weird when we were colleagues," Clyde continues. Dad was on the faculty of the school where Clyde still teaches. That's how they met. Clyde moved in next door later, hoping to land me, as Dad puts it.

"Dad was an excellent teacher," I say.

"Maybe," Clyde says dubiously. "He sure taught some strange topics. Wandered a long way from the text books and the curriculum."

"Like what topics?"

"The details of the effects of malnutrition. Starvation and politics. The details of the effects of exposure to massive

Chapter One

radiation. The economics of nuclear power. The sex life of bees. The sex life of worms. The sex life of *corn!* Dolphins and language. Intelligence and philosophy."

"He's ahead of his time. Too bad the leaders of the world aren't studying those things," I say. "The kids loved it."

"Why'd he quit teaching, then?"

I glare sharply at Clyde. "You know perfectly well school administrators are as stupid as world leaders," I bark. "Now you leave Dad alone!"

But Clyde goes on. "And all the weird stuff he's into now. Meditation. Chanting. Talking to animals. I've seen him with his nose not six inches from the doorway to that *beehive!* And pyramids!"

"His hobbies aren't going to hurt anyone. Quit worrying, and leave him alone." I feel cross.

"I'm not going to get in his way, believe me. It's you I worry about, Marta." He reaches toward me, to touch my arm, but I pull back.

"Don't worry about me. Dad and I'll do fine," I tell him.

* * *

I heard hammering when I arrived home from the office this afternoon and went out back. Dad's putting together some contraption -- all I see at first are some shiny aluminum things and long sticks he's inserting into the openings. "Hi, Marta," he calls, cheery as can be. "How are ya?"

"I'm fine," I say, giving him a little hug. "What're you making now?"

"Watch! You'll see in a minute."

I look more carefully and see that he's salvaged the sticks from the kindling he scrounged from that sawmill where they make wooden molding by the bale. He inserts them one at a time in the openings in the aluminum, and then nails each one fast. "Where'd you get these?" I ask, touching one of the metal pieces.

"Bought a kit at the book store. Look here!" He fastens several of the aluminum thingies together, using his sticks, putting them in without nailing each one. "So you can see what it is," he explains, straining to get the last one to bow a little and fit in place. "See?"

"Yes, I see. It's the outline of a pyramid," I say, feeling the old worry thing in my belly again. Perfectly illogical, I know, but I feel it. "What do you want it for?" It's as tall as he is, now that it's assembled. He's going back and nailing each stick in place. The hammering annoys me, hindering conversation.

"Oh, I dunno. Experiment with it, maybe," he says, full of good cheer.

"Like sharpening razor blades," I offer, scornfully.

"Don't mock, Marta," he chides, still happy as can be. "We'll test it scientifically."

"On razor blades?" I squeal.

"No. I'm more interested in worms. And in myself."

"Worms! What's it gonna do for the worms?"

"Sold a worm bed to a guy this morning. He tells me he went to some conference in California, and one of the fellas there told about an experiment where they put a pyramid over the worm bed and the danged worms grew big as snakes."

I've never been what you could call excited about the worms. That's illogical, too, I know. But I certainly don't relish the idea of worms as big as snakes out in the back yard.

Dad saw my involuntary shudder. "Don't worry, Marta. They won't bother you. We'll just see what we get."

I'm silent. He *is* crazy. Maybe Clyde is right. He nails away, finishing the pyramid. It looks strange -- shiny new aluminum corners, and old weather-beaten molding sticks. But he's proud of it.

"Dad?"

"Yeah, Marta. What?"

"You said you were interested in worms, and in yourself. What about yourself?"

"Well, the most important experiments anyone can perform are on oneself. I'm doing it, more and more. On beyond Mind Games! You know." He winked.

"So what are you gonna do with this thing?"

"I dunno. Meditate under it, probably. For starters. That's

Chapter One 81

why I made it this big. I can get right in here --" He waved his hand in the open space in the middle of the outlined pyramid.
"Oh." I feel small. That's illogical, too. But that's what I feel. "Well," I add lamely, "be careful."
"Sure, I'll be careful," he says. "What's the danger?" he asks, winking again.
"I don't know," I say softly. "But maybe you don't know either."
"I'll be all right. Like you been tellin' Clyde."
"You heard that?"
"You yelled it all over the neighborhood," he says, grinning.
"I did?" I look around, and over toward Clyde's back yard. "I didn't realize." I feel foolish. "I'll go get some supper together," I tell him.
"Sure. Call me. I'll be right here."
So I go in the back door, and get quite a start when I see what's on the kitchen table. A package of little black plastic pyramids, wrapped in clear plastic foil, and several loose ones. I hesitate to touch them. I remember thinking, Marta, you're getting very jumpy. So his latest little hobby is pyramids. Why is that upsetting you? I talk myself out of my strange mood, carry his plastic pyramids to his desk in his room, and start supper.
Later while we're eating, I ask him, "You're really getting into pyramids, aren't you, Dad?"
"Well, I made that one this afternoon, yes. Why?"
"What about all those little black plastic ones?"
He stops chewing. "What about 'em?" he asks, a little warily.
"I never saw 'em before. You left them here on the kitchen table."
"I did? Dang. I never intended to do *that!*"
"Oh?" I ask. "You sound like you wish I hadn't seen them. What's to hide?"
"Oh, nothing," he says, too quickly.
"Where'd you get them?" I ask.
"At the drug store."
"Today?"

"No. I got 'em, on impulse, that day I bought ear stopples."

"Stopples."

"Yeah," he says, grinning. "Don't you love that word? Stopples." He's changing the subject on me again, and I let him, again. "They got two kinds. Wanta see 'em?" He pushes his chair back.

"Not at the supper table."

"Oh." He's stalled. "Maybe later?"

"Sure. And the pyramids?"

"I just picked 'em up for the heck of it."

"What are they for?"

"Uh -- nothing, really. Uh -- no, nothing."

"Something," I say, bearing down on him. He likes the way I do that. No one pulls any fast ones on Marta, I've heard him say. Not even me, he adds, meaning himself. "Something, Dad."

"Nah. Forget about 'em. An old man's toys, is all."

"More experiments?"

"You could say," he mumbles. "Forget 'em."

After supper he tells me more about ear stopples than I thought I needed to know. Although maybe I could make a HUNK O' LOGIC column out of it. If the county can't enforce Ninety-five Decibels, some of us need to do something...

He had little chunks of soft foam, with hard little handles on one end. And pink balls of pliable plastic -- another brand. He wanted me to try 'em, too. He had two pair of each -- he'd tried one set, and wanted me to try the other. "So we can compare notes," he says, excited like a kid.

"Can you hear me?" he asks.

"Yes. It all sounds like we're in a cave," I report.

"What do you hear now?"

"Crackling and popping and gurgling, especially when I move my jaw."

It became a touching, intimate scene -- almost sexy. I mean, Freud would have said it *was* erotic, inserting elongated pink objects into bodily orifices...

"What do you hear now?"

"Voices," I report, thinking of Freud.

Chapter One 83

"That's your roof-brain-chatter!" he crows. "Let's hear it for roof-brain-chatter!"

What's the quietest thing in the world? A flea walking across an elephant's balls with sneakers on. What's the noisiest thing in the world? --

Dad asks me something else. I take it to be, "What do you hear now?" but I can't hear a sound. I yank the stopples out -- "I couldn't hear anything!" I yell.

He roars with laughter. "I fooled ya! I didn't say anything. I just mouthed it -- but it fooled you!"

"So, what have you concluded about ear stopples?" I ask, when we finally stop laughing.

"They don't work worth a damn," he says, sobering. "Motorcycles, and trucks, come barreling right on in, into the inside of my head. There oughta be a law."

"There *is,*" I remind him. "But no one's enforcing it."

Later that evening about bed-time I go out back, looking for him. He's been out an hour or so, doing God-knows-what in the moonlight.

I find him sitting like a yogi cross-legged on a plank across one of the worm beds, under his pyramid. His eyes are closed. He is totally unaware of my presence.

I watch him a while. He doesn't move at all. For a moment I panic -- maybe he's dead! But, no, rigor mortis doesn't set in that quickly -- he'd flop over. He's holding himself up. And he's breathing. I study his chest under his open bathrobe. He's barely breathing. I feel guilty, eavesdropping. Spying, like Clyde.

What an old man! His body is beautiful. The robe is open. I can tell he's quite a magician. He has a mighty magic wand! I see it. I feel like a naughty little girl, peeking, looking. But I see it. How can an innocent young girl *not* see it? It embarrasses me, in the dark. I turn away and come in.

And I sit here and write all this and wonder -- who is he, really? What do I know about him? Am I in any danger? Danger of what? Rape? Absent-mindedness? Love?

How old is he? He was always this old. What is he up to? Whatever it is, he's sure ready for action!

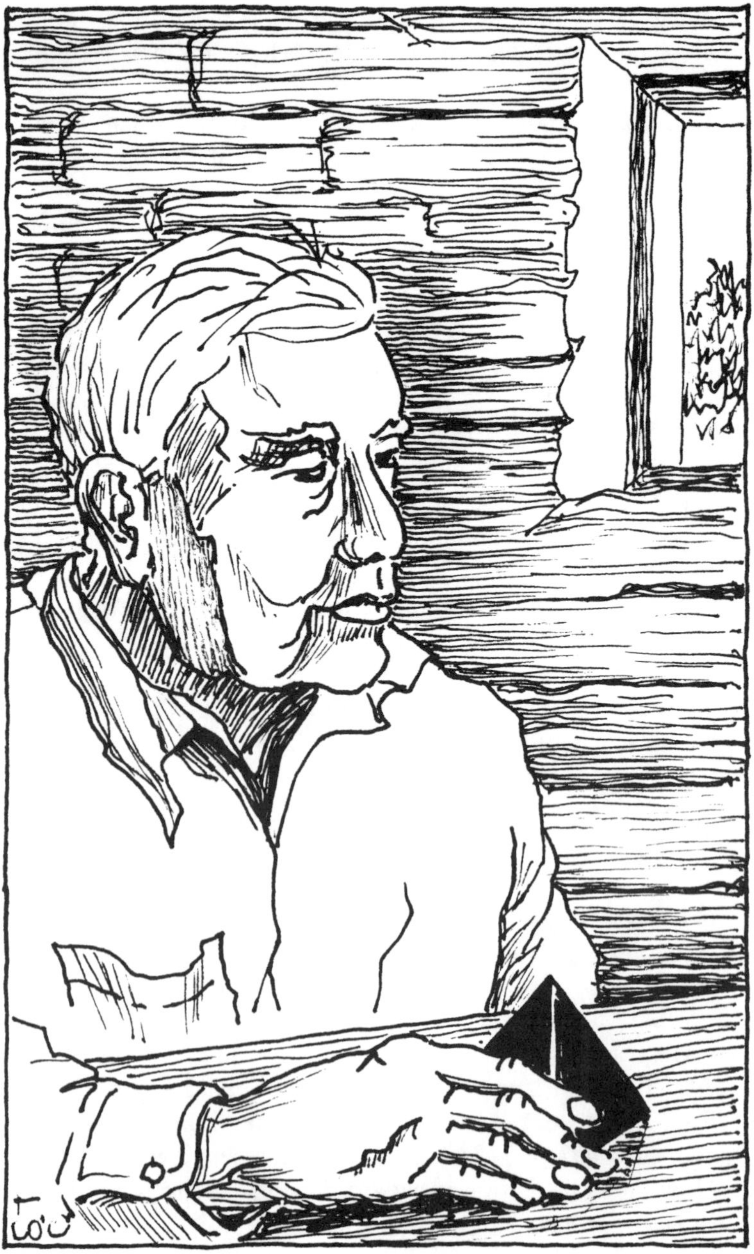

Chapter Two

Strange day in Duke City. I went up in the mountains, to interview the family of a young girl who was attacked by a pack of wild dogs a week ago. On the way back I found the freeway jammed up completely, in the middle of the day. For a while nothing moved. Finally the extreme right lane began inching ahead. It took me an hour to squeeze over, and another hour to stop-and-start my way to the first exit ramp. Half a day gone. And it's hard to get any serious thinking done in the middle of such a mess. You have to waste every minute and every ounce of attention watching for every chance to move an inch.

I arrive home and go to work at my desk. Clyde calls.

"Where are you?" I ask. "I thought we were going downtown for lunch."

"I'm sorry. I been stuck all day in a traffic jam," he explains. "Oh, you, too. I wasted a couple hours there myself. Where are you now?"

"I walked to Candelaria and Edith."

"'Way up there?" I cry. "Why so far?"

"It's the first intersection I came to."

"My God, the traffic jam is three miles from there. I got off at San Pedro." I can't understand why he went so far.

"Well, anyway, here's where I am. Can you come get me?"

"You're on foot?"

"That's what I said!" he yells, losing that infinite patience which frustrated would-be suitors try to keep in place.

"O.K., I'll come get you."

On the way over, I concluded that there had to be two

different major accidents that had caused two huge freeway tie-ups. Might be a HUNK O' LOGIC column in it. I felt bad that I never asked Clyde if his old rattletrap of a car was damaged.

I found him looking quite bedraggled. He pretends to be an athlete, but evidently the waiting and the walking had worn him out. "You all right?" I ask. "Not hurt?"

He seems to like my concern. "No, except I'm mad as hell. Damn car."

"Were you in a wreck?"

"No, I'm barreling along, just fine. And all of a sudden, the damn thing just quits. Motor stops. Won't start. *Will not start*, no matter what I try. I wore the battery down to a low growl, trying."

"Well, you knew it needed work."

"The battery?"

"The whole car! Dad told you that, many a time. Sounds like an airplane, everytime you start it in the morning. He told me he complained to you that you were disturbing him."

"It wasn't that bad," Clyde mumbles.

"It was so! You were definitely in violation of the Ninety-Five Decibel law." I catch myself sounding like Dad, sometimes.

"Well, it doesn't matter," Clyde says. "Now it won't start at all. Zero decibels."

"Serves you right," I smirk at him. "Funny it happened right in the middle of such a traffic jam."

"Yeah."

"Did you see the accident?"

"No. Just a lot of stalled cars in the way of other cars. Goddam mess!"

"Strange."

"I'll have to have it towed, I guess."

"Want to stop downtown? For that lunch?"

"No, thanks. Take me home. I gotta clean up, and figure out what to do." Clyde is really upset. He doesn't like having his day interfered with.

Chapter Two

* * *

Dad was waiting for me, acting a little worried, which is unusual for him. I mean, he knows I may or may not show up for lunch. We have an understanding. If I'm not in by 12:30, he fixes his own. I like the way he wants to try to share meals. Breakfast we always eat together. Supper, too, most evenings. But lunch is not a date, and he knows it.

"Where you been?" he asks.

"Out. Why?" I retort. I don't like the proprietary tone I'm picking up.

"Well, I was worried about you."

"Whatever for?" I ask.

He follows me to my desk. "I dunno," he says. "I'm -- I'm glad you're back. And O.K."

"Of course, I'm O.K." I feel a twinge of that worry thing about *him* again. Why is he fussing over me all of a sudden? Marta can take care of herself, I've heard him tell people, especially Clyde. But he's fretting like a mother hen. "Clyde's car broke down and I went after him," I report. "After I spent most of the morning in my own traffic jam."

I expect him to be relieved, but he's not. "Traffic jam, eh? And Clyde's Lockheed-Boeing broke down?" A fleeting grin crosses Dad's face, but then he resumes fretting. "But you're O.K. Both of you."

"Clyde's plenty upset about the car. Says he'll have to tow it. But, yes, we're O.K. I don't see why you're so upset. Have you had lunch?"

"Not much. Let's have some." He smiles and pats my arm.

Later, we're dawdling at the table, while I try to muster the wherewithal to do some telephoning about all the huge traffic jams in town. Duke City is turning into Los Angeles. Dad seems to be keeping me company, which is a little unusual in the middle of the day.

"Marta?" he says.

"Hmm," I answer, sipping my tea.

"I wanta transfer ownership of this house to you."

"What?"

"The will says it's yours. I don't have anybody else to leave it to. But I want you to have it now, if you want it."

"Dad, you don't have to --"

"I only ask that you let me live here, like a non-paying boarder, maybe --" He lets it dangle.

"Like my Dad," I say.

He's pleased. "Will you drive me to the courthouse this afternoon? Maybe we can take care of it right away, if we go together."

"Sure," I say. "Is there some reason for the hurry?"

"No hurry. I been thinking about it for months, but now I wanta do it. O.K.?"

"Sure. And thank you very much. I mean, you don't have to --"

"I know I don't, but I want to. Let's go."

So we go to the courthouse, and it takes quite a while, but he pushes and pulls and finally it's done. We're driving back and he blurts out, "You ever seen those twenty acres your Mama and I bought outside of Belen?"

"No," I reply.

"I'm giving them to you, too. Let's go see 'em. We'll have to do *that* courthouse bit some other day, being it's so late and in another county, but I'd sure like to show ya that land. Unless you're too busy," he adds.

I thought of the huge traffic jams, and the run-around non-answers I'd be sure to get from the PR desk at the police department, and decided to let the story wait. There may not be a story anyway. I mean, a traffic jam can hardly be the most urgent thing...

"Let's go," I say, grinning at Dad. "You're making me a wealthy landowner."

"Not very. But I want it to be yours."

So we go and see twenty acres that Dad is giving to me. Flat, wind-swept cactus and sage brush and tumbleweeds. Rugged mountains to the east, and the flat horizon fifty miles away to the west. "Hang on to it, if you can, Marta. It'll take care of you later," he says. We're standing close, and he puts an arm around me. I get a little teary, and stand very still until

Chapter Two

I can get control of myself.

On the way back, heading toward Duke City from the south, we're stopped by a police road-block. "Road closed ahead," the cop says.

"What's the trouble, Officer?" I ask.

"Traffic jam. Turn around here."

"Another one!" I exclaim. "I can't believe it! Three in one day! The system is breaking down."

Dad looks a little pale, I think. "Turn around here, Marta, while you still can," he says, echoing the policeman. "What's the cause of the trouble, Officer?" Dad asks.

"Never mind, just keep moving," the cop says gruffly. "Get it turned around, Lady," he growls at me.

"And what route do you recommend for sovereign citizens entering Duke City?" Dad inquires, too politely.

The policeman stops waving his arm and glares at Dad. "Good question, Your Honor. The Police Force humbly recommends taking the extreme left lane of the Interstate at a slow and careful pace. At that it'll take you all evening."

"Thank you very much, Sir" Dad replies.

"Your humble servant," the cop says, and salutes.

I turned around and headed for the freeway. It did take all evening. Dad was fascinated. He wanted the window down, to listen for something, he said, but he wouldn't tell what. I wanted it up, to keep out the cloud of methane exhaust from all the stopped and idling cars.

The experience was not exactly boring, like traffic jams usually are. Dad was as excited as a six-year-old. "What a jam-up! And you say you were in one this morning?"

"And Clyde was in a different one. What do you suppose is going on? Could it be the Russians? Or the Mafia? Or the C.I.A.? I mean, should we be worried?"

"Nah, I don't think so," Dad says, grinning broadly.

"What's so funny?" I ask him.

"Nothing. It just tickles me somehow."

I think maybe I should worry more, about him, if not about the whole international situation. At home I turn on the television. Nothing unusual about the world news. Same old chronic disasters. Local stories of murders, jury trials, fires. Helicopter traffic report. "An unusual number of obstructions on the interstates and on major arteries in all sections of town." Reporter sounded almost as frantic as when he was selling unpainted furniture. Nothing special, didn't seem like.

* * *

After a late supper I called the PR department of the police. I couldn't get through to anybody, so I decided to let it go. Nice thing about a column is I don't have to chase sirens to get stories while they're hot. And I'm still not even sure traffic jams can be made into much of a story.

After my bath, I went to the kitchen door and looked out into the dark. It seemed so peaceful. A jet-liner was landing, but it was just coasting quietly. "C'mon out," Dad says, startling me. "Enjoy it with me a minute."

I go out and find him flopped in our lounge chair in his robe. I sit in a lawn chair. "I didn't know you spent much time here," I say.

"Usually it's too noisy to be much fun," he says. "But it's nice tonight. We can hear the crickets. There's a big toad over there under that trumpet vine. He'll startle you, if you don't know he's there." Dad was wallowing in his pleasure.

"How's the traffic out front?" I ask. Usually it's so noisy it prevents conversation in our back patio.

"It's there, but it's not too loud," Dad says. "I can live with that." We listened a while. Swish, swish-swish, shush, shush-shush. It was not offensive. "I think of it like surf," Dad says.

"Surf."

"The one thing Duke City lacks that it really needs is an ocean," he asserts flatly. "But that sound of humanity passing our door, now that it's quieted down, is almost soothing. Like surf, at the ocean."

"Oh." I'm not an ocean addict.

"Here we are, listening to the surf of the sea of humanity," Dad says.

"Are you a poet, too?" I ask him.

Chapter Two

"Too?"

"Well, you're a teacher. And a -- a magician." I blush in the dark, remembering his wand, and am glad I don't have to explain. "Now you sound like a poet."

"I don't understand modern poetry," he states.

We're silent a good while, and the crickets and the shushing traffic soothe us. "Dad," I ask finally, "why did you come here?"

"To marry your mother," he replies instantly.

"You knew her before you moved out here from back East?"

"No. But that's the reason I came," he says.

"Well, why did you leave where you came from?"

He's silent a long time. I imagine weird and horrible things, like he killed somebody, or embezzled a million dollars, or something. I'm not sure he's going to answer. The toad moves, and I'm watching it, in silence.

"I had to go somewhere," Dad says quietly.

"Dad, you don't have to tell me, if you don't want to. I was just thinking, you're a pretty amazing person, and -- and I like you, and you've been wonderful to me. Today's more evidence of that -- house and land, and -- and our companionship, here." I'm getting embarrassed again, for no logical reason. "I just realized that there's a lot about you that I don't know."

"Yes, that's so."

I decide not to pry any further. He can tell me if he wants to. I guess it doesn't really matter. We sit in silence a long time. I'm about to get up and go in and go to bed, when he says, "Maybe it's part of my answer to the first big question."

"What do you want?" I quote it back to him.

"Yes. I love that about you, Marta, that you don't forget. You're paying attention when someone tells you something, and you remember."

"Peace and quiet." I quote his answer to the question.

"Yes." He doesn't speak for a while. "I was a queer person back there. For a long time."

"Queer," I echo. Surely not. He's hetero all the way, if I know anything at all about that business.

"Strange. Peculiar. A little off, everybody thought."

"Oh, that kind of queer," I say aloud. "How so?"

"I lived all alone, out on the edge of town, in a shack surrounded by empty fields. None of the modern conveniences that are so important to everybody. No electricity. A pump in the yard for water. Horses and wagons, instead of a car or a truck."

He begins to talk faster. "I minded my own business. Hauled cans and ashes in a horse-drawn wagon. All through the Depression and the War. Kids teased me, threw stones at me and the horses. Said I was crazy."

"Why was an educated man like you living like that?"

"I wasn't educated. I was living the only way I knew how, and not keeping up with the times at all. I *was* a little crazy, maybe."

"You're a schoolteacher!" I exclaim. "You have a fistful of what you call worthless degrees!"

"All those are from after I came out here. I like that about the west. An old feller can go to the University, and no one says, 'You can't come here, Old Man -- you're too old. You're queer!'"

"How old *are* you, Dad?" I ask suddenly. He must be even older than I thought.

"Gettin' up there," he says, and I can hear the grin in his voice.

"So, why'd you have to leave? The teasing?"

"It was kinda like that, only the grown-ups did it." He doesn't speak, and I'm ready to accept that he's not going to tell any more. Then he starts in again. "After the war all the fields around my place were subdivided, streets laid out, curbs, sidewalks, new little houses, lawns, fenced-in gardens. All that 'growth' --" He spits out the last word.

"The town grew."

"The neat little people in their neat little houses surrounded me, on all sides. There I was in a tar-paper shack. Outdoor privy. Pot-bellied stove. One kid used to visit me, friendly-like, and said my place was warmer than his folks', and they had a coal furnace in the cellar! But my place looked like a trash pile, compared to the new little painted houses. Sheds, wagons,

Chapter Two

wood-pile, manure pile!" He stops briefly.

"Well, they wanted me to move. Where was I gonna go? I didn't have the cash for the paving assessment, and it didn't do any good for me to protest that I didn't *want* the street paved. I didn't want the street at all!"

"So, what happened?" I urge, when he stops again.

"The more they moved in, the more my place went up in value. I didn't wanta go anywhere at all, but after a while I could see that they were ready to get nasty. They were afraid of fire at my place, they said. And they became so mean, I was afraid, too, finally. I heard talk of settin' fire to my woodpile and lettin' it spread. And some of them were urging the town council to sell my place out from under me, for the paving assessment.

"I finally got a little help. The kid with the coal furnace advised me, and did the leg work. He and his dad came up with a figure, a little high, they assured me -- and they offered my place to the four neighbors who surrounded me. They split it four ways and paid me cash. I often wondered later how in hell they came up with that kind of money. Second mortgages, no doubt. Wanted me out that bad.

"Paid me for everything, as is, where is. But I fooled 'em. Instead o' trying an apartment downtown, I got on a train and never looked back. Landed here."

"You never went back."

"Nope."

"Never heard again from anybody?"

"My young coal furnace buddy was killed in Korea."

"But, you've become a different person. That story hardly sounds like you at all," I say, more and more surprised as his tale sinks in. "How'd you find the U.? And Mama?"

"That's another story," he says, sounding weary. "You wanted to know why I came -- and now I've told you. To find peace and quiet. That's all I want."

We listened to the night sounds, and traffic shushing by out front. "The interference here has been getting to me -- like they're gonna cut me up and throw the pieces in all directions, all over again. But maybe we can head 'em off, Marta. We'll sure have a good time trying!"

I didn't pretend to understand what he meant. Sometimes I go back to nearly full-time worrying about him. He *is* crazy. His whole story is crazy. I even wonder if it's true, now that I'm not listening to him tell it. I mean, how could it be?

It *is* quieter tonight, however, than it has been in our neighborhood in a very long time.

* * *

I received a call at the office from Clyde, even though I told him not to do that except in case of emergency, because he used to pester me so much. "You all right?" I ask when the telephone secretary tells me who's on the line.

"Sure," he says. "But I just heard something I think may interest you."

"What is it? Where are you? Is Dad all right?"

"Far as I know," says Clyde. "I'm at school. We were listening to KTLK, waiting for the sports news --"

"Oh, yes," I growl. Clyde listens to the radio talk station because he's like the rest of those athletic-minded teachers at that school. "Most comprehensive sports news in Duke City." So he listens to all that garbage people call in, just to get the ball scores. "So what did you hear?" I ask, a little harshly.

"You know that traffic jam you were in? And the one I was in? They weren't the same one."

"I figured as much," I say, more interested than I expected to be. "Dad and I were in another one last night. Actually, we were turned back by the police *before* we got in it."

"And do the cops have any explanation today?" Clyde asks.

"They're less co-operative and less informative than usual," I tell him. "Which means they're really stumped and the PR department has no idea what to say. They're just telling callers which sections of town to try to avoid."

"But it's all over the city!"

"More or less," I admit. "You said you heard something."

"Yeah. Lady called in. Said she thought the explanation might be in the want-ads in last Sunday's paper. You got 'em

there?"
"I can get them."
"Take a look," he says. "The lady read this one over the air, and I'm sure you'll be interested. I heard it just once. I remember the first words were, 'Beginning next Wednesday...'"
"Hold on a minute." I ask the secretary to get me a copy of last Sunday's paper. For once I'm not embarrassed or ticked at Clyde's call. Usually he's a pain, but this time I'm curious. "What kind of want-ad was it, Clyde? There are two whole sections of 'em in this paper."
"I remember she said it was in 'personals.'"
"Aha!" I reply, teasing. "In with the escort services and massage parlors."
"You got it, Marta," he says with a laugh. "I'm sure the first word was 'beginning.'"
I finger down through the AAA escorts and the AA escort and the A-1 massages. Early in the B's I find it. "Here it is. 'Beginning on Wednesday.'"
"Read it, and tell me what you think."
I read aloud. *"Beginning on Wednesday morning, if your vehicle does not have a muffler which muffles to a level below ninety-five decibels, the motor will not function in Duke City. Replace the muffler, so that your vehicle is not in violation."*
"That's all?" Clyde asks, after I'm silent a second.
"That's it."
"Well, whaddaya think?" he asks.
"I don't think anything. It's stupid."
"Oh, really? I thought you'd think it was worth checking out. I'm sure going to."
"Check it out? How, Clyde?" I'm getting the old impatient-with-Clyde feeling again.
"I'm gonna get a new muffler!"
"Well, you sure as hell needed one."
"I know. Mr. Myers told me that often enough."
"Let me know how it works," I say, but I'm unenthusiastic.
"I sure will. See you!" he answers cheerily.
I work a while on my next HUNK O' LOGIC, and then decide to go home early in order to miss the rush hour down

town. I'm almost home, and a police roadblock stops me. Another traffic jam! Right at our place! A policeman is trying to detour me around. "I live just half a block down there," I tell him.

"Park it and walk, Lady. And be careful."

I lock the car behind the carwash and walk to the policeman. "What's causing all these traffic jams?" I ask him.

"Bad accident. Please be careful, Lady. Wires down. Detour, Mister! No way through!"

I work my way past the curious onlookers and the parked cars and ambulances and firetrucks and electric company repair trucks. Police cars with their blinking red lights are all around. The center of the storm is nearly across from our place. I see Dad out in front, talking to a policeman with a clipboard.

"You saw the cause of the accident, Sir?" the policeman asks politely.

"I sure did, and it was no accident!" Dad yells, excited. "Oh, Hi, Marta," he says, grinning, and gives me a little hug. "What a mess!" He waves his arm across the street.

A car has shivered an electric company pole to splinters and severed it at ground level. Several wires hold it as it sways freely. A car with smashed front end and crushed hood and windshield huddles beyond the pole. Electric company linemen are climbing on other poles up and down the street, while rescue squad people watch. The police are blocking traffic.

"What happened, Sir?" the policeman asks Dad.

"I was out here gathering up the daily peck o' trash that people throw on my place." He opens a grocery sack he has in his hand. "Bottles, cans, wrappers, even dirty diapers -- see! I come out every day and clean up their shit."

The policeman is eyeing Dad in a funny way. "The wreck, Sir?"

"Yeah. The guy ridin' shotgun there threw a beer bottle out the window. I saw him -- he tossed it up and out --" Dad makes a lifting gesture with his arm and hand. "Damn litterer! Filthy --" The policeman is putting his pencil into his shirt pocket, as if Dad's testimony isn't interesting him much.

"Damn bottle bounced under the car and broke and the guy

Chapter Two 97

ran over it and it blew one of his paper-thin tires! Look at 'em! And the driver's drunk as a lord! You checked that out already, surely."

"I'm interested in the accident, Sir. The cause of it. I don't need any lectures," the policeman says and steps away. Dad follows him, yelling. "He blew a tire and swerved and plowed into the pole! But it wasn't an accident!"

The policeman wheels on Dad and suddenly they're nose to nose. "Not an accident? Then what the hell was it?"

"That guy didn't throw the beer bottle by accident! It was very deliberate. I saw him, grinning at me as he chucked it! And the driver didn't get going fifty miles an hour with bald tires in a thirty-five mile zone by accident! And he didn't get drunk by accident! They did all that on purpose!"

"You're crazy, Old Man. Go home and try and stay out of trouble!" the policeman barks. He walks away, leaving Dad standing there with his mouth open.

"I'll be damned," Dad says, finally. "And I probably saved their worthless lives." He's musing, halfway to himself. "Hot wires flashin' and poppin' and flyin' around like snakes --" He turns and says to me, "And those drunken litterers too far gone to think straight. I have to yell at 'em to stay in the car and not touch anything 'til the Electric Company gets here." He glares at all the rescue activity. "That's all the thanks a body gets. They probably won't even give 'em a ticket for smashing the pole. The rest of us'll get to pay for it on the next electric bill."

* * *

Last night I was yanked out of sleep and a dream of soothing seaside surf by the squeal of brakes and a tremendous metallic crash, followed by the tinkling and clinking of falling glass. Another car wreck! They're common, one must say, on Isidro Boulevard. Friday and Saturday nights are especially bad, we've noticed. Sometimes Dad jokes about it. "Here we are on our Saturday night date in our own living room, and the entertainment hasn't shown up yet!"

We went to bed early last night. He was weary from

shoveling compost and feeding wormbeds by the wheelbarrowload -- and I had had a hard day at the office. The Boss wasn't interested in my HUNK O' LOGIC on mufflers and traffic jams. Said it was *not* logic. Said it was silly. I couldn't get anywhere arguing with him. But it all went out of my mind when I went to bed. I must have fallen asleep immediately.

The crash brought me rearing up out of the bed. I grab my robe and call to Dad from the hall. "Dad!"

His bedroom/study door is open. "What?" he asks, sounding bored.

"There's been a wreck out front!"

"I heard it. Another one."

"Sounded serious. The noise was awful."

"Yep. Woke me up."

He hasn't moved in the bed. I step into his room. "You O.K.?" I ask.

He raises his head. "I *was* O.K. I was fine, doing my -- my work. I was busy. Someone could maybe say I was sleeping, but I am not idle while I sleep. I was doing the work. And now -- I have been interrupted. So -- no, I am *not* O.K!"

"You're not getting up?"

"Getting up? What for?"

"To check on the accident. To see if anyone is hurt. To call the police. To call an ambulance, probably."

"No, thanks."

"What do you mean, 'No, thanks'?" I squeal. "Somebody may be hurt badly."

"Somebody is almost certainly drunk. And now the predictable consequences of that irrational behavior have come to pass. Chickens come home to roost. And my life, my work is disturbed."

"So, let's go see if we can help," I say.

"Help! What's helpful about summoning a dozen screaming sirens and spotlights and loudspeakers -- and giving away blankets, and getting our living room rug all bloody and muddy by people making phone calls? We've done all that, Marta. It doesn't *help!*"

"You're not getting up? Someone may be dying out there!"

Chapter Two

"If it's the drunken driver, *that* might help. A little."
"I can't believe you."
"I'm tired of it, Marta. We're not helpers out there in the street. We're victims -- of the interference!"
I become angry. "You sound like you think somebody deliberately figured out how to do something that would disturb your little project -- your crazy magic -- your dreams and sleep and selfish thoughts and wild ideas! You're crazy! I worry about you!"
"Don't," he says.
"Some poor bastard got drunk, because he's miserable. He's not thinking of you! He's not trying to interfere with *you!* He doesn't give a damn about you at all!"
"Well, I'm returning the compliment this time," Dad says, and rolls over in bed away from me.
"Your peace and quiet stinks!" I yell at him, and yank his door shut after me as I go out.
The driver *was* drunk. Barrelling up the wrong side of the road, he plowed into a parked truck. Demolished truck and car. Police reported, "D.O.A." They didn't need Dad, or me. Just clean up the mess. Be thankful there were no passengers this time. Somebody lost a truck through no fault of his own. Parked it on a boulevard that drunks insist on using. The owner can be thankful he wasn't in his truck when the drunk claimed it.

* * *

Clyde told me he had his car towed to a shop and had a new muffler put on and drove it home with no problem.
"Doesn't make sense," he says to me, "but there's no denying it. It wouldn't work before. I put the new muffler on, which cost me quite a bit. But that's absolutely all I did to it, and it works fine now."
But the Boss wouldn't even listen. "It's nonsense, Marta. The muffler isn't what makes the motor run, or not run. Now get off that horseshit and bring me something serious. HUNK O' LOGIC, indeed!"

I drove over to San Rafael Park. Lowriders and motorcyclists frequent the area, and think of it as theirs, really. I'm not sure exactly what I was looking for.

Three young men were sitting under a tree smoking, a little distance from three parked motorcycles. I walk up to them. "Nice day," I say, smiling sweetly.

"Sure, Lady. Nice day." They look at each other, after examining me warily.

"Listen, I'm a reporter, and I'm trying to find out --"

"We don't talk to no reporters, Lady," one says. "We learned our lesson."

"Yeah," says another. "We don't want no trouble."

"Oh, this isn't going to cause any trouble," I say quickly, trying to assure them. "I wanted to ask about your bikes, there."

"What about 'em?"

"Any trouble with them lately? Getting them to run? Getting the motors started, I mean?"

They eye each other carefully. "How'd you know?" one asks me, and then he has to grin.

"Manny was off his wheels for a coupla days, 'til we figured it out," another one says.

"Tell me about it, Manny," I ask him.

"Not much to tell. Got up one day and it wouldn't start. Called Joe, here, and he couldn't start it, either. Some of the other guys in the gang had the same kinda trouble. I was really pissed. These guys thought it was funny." The other two are grinning broadly.

"But your bike runs now," I say.

"Yeah. We figured it out."

"What did you figure out?"

"Put the guts back in," Manny says.

"Tell me what that means."

"Some of us pulled the guts out of our mufflers. Little bit better gas mileage. Lots o' noise. Feels good. Tough, you know. Power!" He made a fist and waved it, grinning.

"Yes. I see. And when you put back -- something --"

"The baffle. No problem."

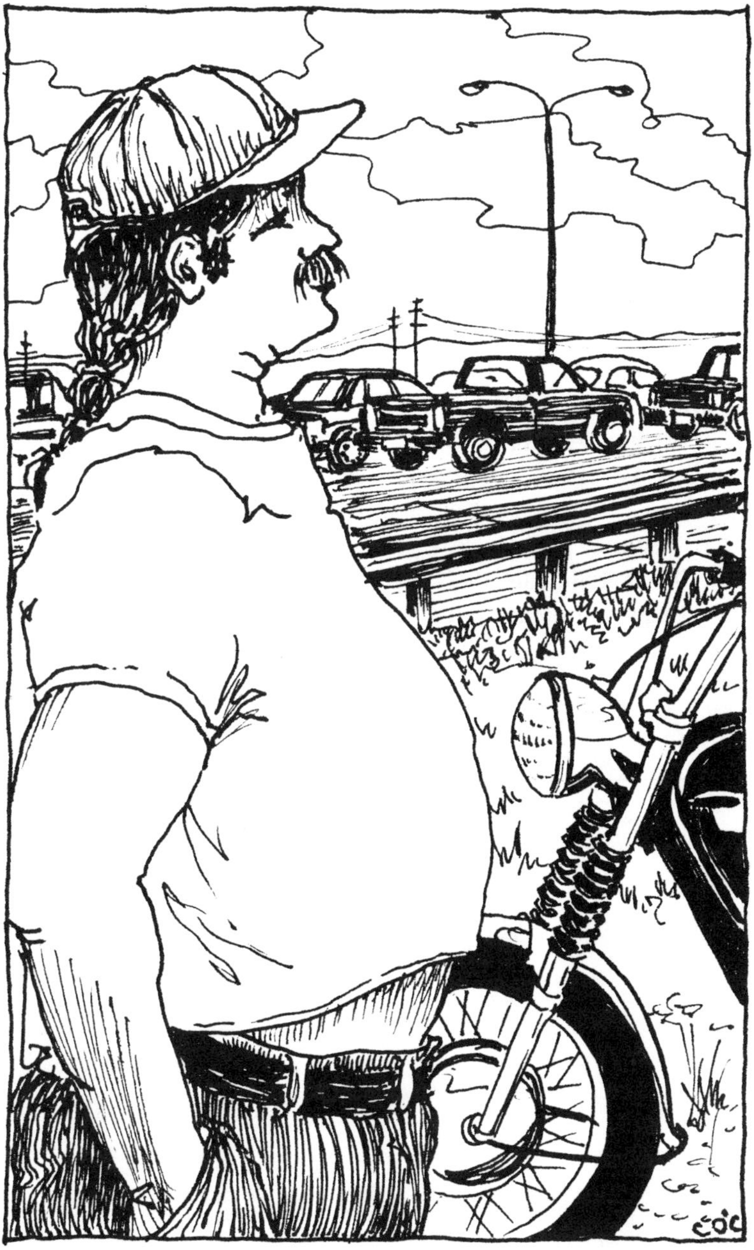

"What made you think of that?"

"The gang was all together. Ridin' double, since about half the bikes wouldn't run. Somebody noticed how much quieter it was. All the loudest bikes were broke down."

"Manny thought of it first."

I grin at them. "So everything's fine, now? As long as your muffler really muffles?"

"Seems so."

We look at each other, and then at the bikes. Then Manny speaks again. "Funny thing about it, though. I mean, besides the fact that it don't make sense." We all laugh.

"What's funny about it?" I ask.

"It's only here in Duke City. This -- this, uh -- hell, I don't know what to call it. But it isn't in Bernalillo. Or Belen. Those guys don't have to have the guts in. Unless they come to Duke City. Then they get stopped in the traffic jams, just inside o' town. So they cool off a while, and put the baffles back in, and then they go on fine."

"What could cause it?" I ask.

"Beats hell outa me, Lady."

* * *

Chapter Three

Things have quieted down. The police announced on the TV news that motorists driving in Duke City would find that they must have mufflers which muffle. Drivers attempting to enter Duke City without functioning mufflers would be stopped near the edge of town. The announcement didn't make clear who or what would stop them. The City Council passed an ordinance increasing the fines for obstructing traffic.

I received a telephone call from Clyde at dawn one morning. "Sorry to bother you so early, Marta. I need a ride. Car broke down again."

"Sure," I answer. "Come on over and I'll take you to school."

"No, I'm not at home. I've been out here all night. I waited to call 'til I thought you'd be up."

"Where are you?"

"Golden Inn."

"My God --" It's an hour's drive, over on the other side of the mountains. "O.K. But you'll be late for school."

"I know. But I didn't wanta bother you any earlier."

So I drove to Golden, to the country music night club. The parking lot was full of cars, which seemed odd so early in the morning. A few were pulling away as I drove in.

Clyde was waiting for me beside the highway. "Hi, Marta," he says. "You're not gonna believe this."

"That your wreck of a car broke down again? Sure, I am. You ought to trade it in."

"No, listen to this."

"Get in. You can tell me while I drive you back."

"I don't need a ride after all," he says, a little sheepishly.

"Don't need a ride? I don't understand."

"I don't either. Lemme tell you what happened. I drove out here to listen to the Jug Band. Remember? I invited you, but you couldn't come. One of the players teaches with me at the school. They're really good. We were drinkin' beer and enjoyin' the hell out of it -- 'til closing time. Then we came out, and no one could get his car started. We were all stuck, except the gal that plays the washboard for the jug band. The band all piled in her car and drove off. And the customers just stood around in the parking lot. No one could get a car started."

"How can it be everybody's car at once?" I ask. "Mufflers! You all need new mufflers!"

"You know I just got a new muffler, and so did half a dozen other guys!"

"So you spent the night out here in the parking lot?"

"The owners locked up and left. I didn't sleep much, and called you at the first daylight."

"You sure did. But now you tell me you don't need a ride," I say, a little cross.

"That's right. Damn thing started a coupla minutes ago and runs fine. Same for some of the other cars. See! They're leaving."

"What was the matter last night?"

"I sure don't know. But it wasn't just *my* car -- it was all of 'em." He looks at me, pleading. "I'm sure sorry, Marta. Sorry to bother you and drag you all the way out here."

"Yeah, well, I am, too," I say. "So you're O.K. now? You don't need me, then?"

"No. I'll drive on in, since the car's working fine."

"O.K. See you." I begin to pull away.

"Sorry, Marta!" he calls after me.

I was really cross. Clyde has become a colossal pain. "A pain where a pill won't reach," Dad would say.

I drove a little way, feeling mostly angry at stupid Clyde, before I realized that I was going on *beyond* Golden, instead of heading back toward Duke City. I decided to continue, and

Chapter Three

make a circle and return to town on the main north-south freeway. A couple of miles beyond Golden I came to a gaggle of cars and pick-ups, all heading toward me, stopped beside the highway. It looked almost like an impromptu meeting. Some of the vehicles were still on the south-bound lane, not well-parked. As I drove by slowly, I noticed people sleeping in some of the vehicles. It was strange. Not exactly a traffic jam, but what could become the beginnings of one.

Later, over on the freeway, I was thick in the commuter traffic coming down from Santa Fe, and found myself in another similar tangle of parked cars, heading south as I was. One lane was open, moving slowly. Police were investigating the stalled cars. I got through it and stopped and walked back.

A policeman was knocking on the window of a parked car. "Open up, Mister! Wake up!" As the car window is lowered, the policeman jerks his head back suddenly. "What's the trouble, Mister?" I'm close enough to hear it all.

"Oooh, my head!" the driver moans.

"You had too many last night, Mister!" the cop says.

"Yeah, I guess so," the man groans.

"You needed to stop, I must say, but why'd you stop here?" the policeman asks. "You shouldn'ta been driving in that condition."

"Car stopped. Wouldn't run. Couldn't start it."

"You were too drunk to tell what you were doing," the cop suggests.

"No, it stalled, and wouldn't start. So I lay down and musta passed out."

"Probably a good thing. But not out here on the freeway," the cop says.

"No, I needed to get home."

"See if it will start now," the cop orders. "We need to clear this area."

The hungover man sits up a little straighter and works foot pedals and turns the ignition key. The motor roars to life. "Works fine, now," the man says. His smile is a grimace. "Oooh, my head."

"Get going, Mister. And be careful," the cop says, stepping

back and waving his hand.
"Excuse me, Officer," I say, showing my press card. "Could I ask you a question, please?"
"Not a good time, Lady. I gotta clear this area."
"I know. Just a second. What's causing all the stalled cars?"
"That I don't know. Most of 'em are able to get going now."
"Do you know of other places where this is happening?"
"Radio says there's a jam-up like this south of town. And another one up in the canyon. And another out near Rio Puerco." He waves his hand at the western horizon.
"I passed something like it, not so big, over near Golden," I say.
"I'm not surprised. But it's strange. Every driver is hungover."
"No kidding! Well, thanks, Officer," I call after him, as he's walking away to confront the driver of the next stalled car.

* * *

This evening Dad and I were sitting in the living room, reading quietly, listening to Mozart. He got up and went to the front door and looked out. We could hear the shush-shush of the surf of the sea of humanity. He turns to me and asks, "Wanta take a walk around the neighborhood?"
"Walk?" I ask. We never walk on Isidro Boulevard. It's too noisy, too dangerous, especially on a Saturday night.
"Doesn't look like the entertainment's gonna come to us. Let's go find it," he proposes, grinning broadly.
"I could stand a little exercise," I say. "Why not? Let's take a walk."
We locked up the house and strolled out on the street. The traffic was almost sedate in its passing. We hiked a block or so, and approached a commotion of yelling and screaming people, in the parking lot of a busy tavern.
"Get Rolando!" a man hollers, as he yanks his head out from under the open hood of a car. "Get him out here!"

Chapter Three

A man in a white apron yells out the open door of the tavern, "Who the hell wants me?"

"I do!" the man at the car screams.

"What's the matter?" Rolando yells. "And quit screaming, Mike."

"Somebody sabotaged my brand new Caddie!" Mike yells.

"What's that to me?" Rolando yells back.

"You need a guard out here to watch this goddamed parking lot!"

Other people standing around agree. "Yeah, Rolando. Mine won't start either."

"Mine either."

Rolando glares at them all. "What am I supposed to do? Your car's a wreck, Carlos. It ain't my fault the damn thing won't start."

"Somebody messed up *all* these cars!" Carlos screams. "And it's your fault. You just wanta keep us here all night. And my old lady wants to go to the Music Box, where they got dancing. Your place is a dump!"

"Well, go away, then!" Rolando barks.

"We'll call the cops!" Carlos calls.

"I'll call the cops!" yells Rolando, and he ducks inside the tavern.

"Damn bastard!" Mike yells. "You'll pay for this."

"Let's go dancin'," a woman drools, leaning over the hood of one of the cars.

"I gotta get home, Mike. The old man'll be furious," dribbles another drunken female from the front seat of Mike's Cadillac.

"The damn cars won't start," growls Mike, disgusted. "There's nothin' I can do. Try it yourself and see."

The worried lady slides over, bumping her head on the steering wheel in the process. "Lemme try," she moans. After a long delay, the starter turns over, but the motor does not start.

"Someone's been messin' with all the cars. It was that bastard Rolando, I think."

Dad's been edging closer to this discussion, very much interested in every word. When a siren sounds in the distance,

I pull on his arm. "C'mon. Let's get away. There's going to be trouble."

"No," he objects. "Let's stay and see. Might be a story here for you, Marta."

Drunks who can't get their cars started didn't seem like much of a story, but Dad really wanted to stay. And I thought of Clyde's troubles that morning.

A police car drives up, and a young officer gets out. "What's the trouble here?"

"Someone's been messin' with our cars while we were inside," explains Mike, still yelling. "Now they won't start. It's goddam Rolando's fault!"

"Have you called a mechanic?" the policeman asks.

"I gotta get home!" Mike's date wails. "I'll get *killed!*"

"It's Rolando's fault," Carlos repeated. *"He* should fix 'em."

"What's the trouble?" the policeman asks again.

"Won't start! Here, you try it," Mike offers. "Slide over," he orders the worried drunk woman inside.

The policeman gasps loudly for air as he climbs into the car. He leaves the door open. He turns the ignition and the brand new Cadillac starts immediately. He looks at Mike. "What's the matter with it?" he asks.

"I'll be damned. It wouldn't do that for me. Or her!" Mike gasps wide-eyed.

"Well, you better get going, then," the policeman says, getting out. "Before there's trouble."

Mike gets in and the motor stops. "Dammit!" he yells.

"What did you do?" his date wails. "I gotta get home, or I'll get killed. We'll *both* get killed."

"I didn't do nothin'!" Mike yells. "I just got in, and it stopped." He grinds the starter, but the motor will not run.

"Oh, my God!" Mike's date laments. "We'll be killed."

"Shut up that broken record," Mike barks. "See, Officer. Something's the matter. I can't make it run. Rolando's been messing with it."

Before I can stop him, Dad steps forward and says sweetly, "May I help?"

Chapter Three 109

"Who in hell are you, Old Man?" Mike growls.
"A sovereign citizen, just passing by. I heard your troubles."
"How can you help?" the policeman asks. "You a mechanic?"
"I'll drive the lady home. You follow me and bring me back. I live a block away, up Isidro Boulevard."
"If I can't make it run, how in hell can you?" Mike asks gruffly. "Unless you're a mechanic."
"I'm not, but *you* had it running," Dad says to the policeman.
"Let him try it," the policeman orders Mike.
Mike climbs out and Dad gets in. The motor starts immediately. Dad smiles generously. "O.K.?" he says to them all.
"Goddam," Mike yelps. "Let me try it again."
"No!" squalls the woman beside Dad. "Just get me home."
"Get in the back, Mister," the policeman says to Mike. "I'll follow you," he adds to Dad.
"You comin', Marta?" Dad calls to me.
"No, thanks. But you be careful," I call.
"I'm all right," Dad croons. "See you in a minute."
I walked home, feeling somehow abandoned by my walking companion.

* * *

Clyde begged me to go to a Sunday afternoon faculty party with him. I wasn't much in the mood, but wanted to get out of the house. Dad was in a strange state, and was making me nervous. I couldn't put my finger on it, but he paced in the living room restlessly. Twice he went out front and, so help me, he was watching the traffic! Once he asked if I wanted to go for a walk, but I declined.
"What ails you?" I ask him, finally. "You're nervous as a hen with ducklings."
"I'm fine."
"Go out back and shovel compost for a while. Burn off some of that energy. You're making me jumpy."

"Might be a good idea," he says.
"I'm going out with Clyde," I tell him.
"Hmp. Well, be careful," he says, and then breaks into a broad grin and claps his hands once. "Ha! As if I had to worry about Marta and that pip-squeak."
"Should I worry about *you?* That's the question. Clyde thinks you're crazy, you know."
"Yeah, I know. A lot of Clyde's thinking is cock-eyed. Don't waste too much of yourself on him, Marta."
"I'm going to a party."
"Have a nice time," he says, with a tinge of sarcasm in his voice, as he goes out the kitchen door.

The party was not really my idea of a good time. Ballgame scores were the chief topic of conversation. There was a midsummer exhibition football game on TV, which some were watching. From time to time it was switched to a baseball game, but nothing was happening there at all except two grown men throwing a ball back and forth.

I held a glass of wine all afternoon. Actually half a glass puts me into the altered state. A little like Mind Games. I sail up into a ceiling corner of the room and watch the proceedings from there in a very detached way, as in certain dreams. And the wine behaves something like truth serum. I see truth -- I hear the true meaning of what is said, if there *is* any true meaning.

That young lady is a dangerous predator. That fellow wonders why I came with Clyde. That woman is surprised that a chicana was allowed into this private party at all. That man -- well, ball scores don't contain much meaning, so I don't learn much about some people.

Clyde and some others were drinking tequila sunrises, and the host ran out of orange juice. No one felt like going out for more. They'd had plenty, anyway, I thought. They substituted Tang for orange juice. Clyde became silly. He sat on the hassock in front of me and made faces at the TV. He stuck his tongue out and rolled his eyes. Some of the faculty wives who were fairly well smashed themselves thought he was cute.

"That face is funny," Clyde accuses the TV image.

Chapter Three

"Your face is funny!" a lush young thing squeals at Clyde. I was coming down from my little half-a-glass-of-wine trip and the whole situation was boring me. I went and poured coffee, for Clyde and me. "Here. Drink this," I tell him. "Sober up enough, so you can take me home."

"Oh? Are you ready to go?" he asks.

"Yes. I'm ready to go," I repeat patiently.

A couple of cups of coffee later, we go through the good-bye routine and leave. Clyde wobbles to the car. "You all right?" I ask him.

"Not really. That Tang isn't settling well."

"Tang!" I snort. "Can you drive?"

"Sure I can drive," he assures me.

But he can't start the car. The starter motor whirrs, but the engine does not fire and go. "You're still drunk," I say to him.

"I am not! This damn car -- I *will* have to trade it in, like you said," he mumbles.

"Let me try it," I say, getting out.

He slides over with a moan. "Ohh, that damn Tang'll kill ya."

"Your problem isn't Tang," I growl. The car starts fine. "Want me to drive home?" I offer.

"Naw, I can drive it," Clyde says, but he doesn't move.

I get out and walk around. When I get to the other side, he's behind the wheel and the motor isn't running. "What'd you do to it?" I bark at him.

"Nothing! I just slid over! Never touched a thing! Oooh, my head. That damn Tang. I'll never drink it again. I guess you better drive, Marta."

So I got back in and the motor started fine and I drove home. My "dates" aren't working out very well lately. By the time I parked in Clyde's driveway, he was passed out. I left him snoring in his car and walked home.

* * *

Dad was on the phone when I went in. He sounded excited. I only heard his end of it, of course.

"This *is* an emergency! If we don't get this stopped, we'll all drown in our own shit. But I caught him. I have his license number -- ATZ-409! I'm reporting a crime. I'm reporting information needed to find and apprehend the criminal. I'm accusing --

"Yes, I'll sign a complaint! Yes, I'll testify in court! Yes! I want the littering stopped... What do you mean, you can't do anything? I see signs all up and down the highway, signs paid for by us sovereign citizens. *'One Hundred Dollar Fine for Throwing Trash on Highway.'* It oughta be a thousand! But what good is the sign, if there's nothing you can do?...

"I tell you, I watched a man throw a beer can on my front lawn, and I have the license number of the car he threw it from! ... When? ... Tomorrow. I'll be here. If I don't answer the doorbell, tell him to go 'round the back and yell. I'll be in my back yard."

He lay the phone down very slowly. He went to his room in a kind of dream state. On beyond Mind Games. I was amazed at how quickly he changed from the animated telephone conversation to a kind of sleep-walking. I can't quit worrying about him.

* * *

I called Clyde next morning, plenty early. "You awake?" I ask, feeling very chipper myself.

"Ooh! Barely, Marta," he answers. "What's going on so early?"

"I found a want-ad, and thought you might be interested. But maybe you're not awake enough yet to handle it."

"Uh -- try me," Clyde mumbles.

"Here it is. In personals. Last Tuesday. Should I read it?"

"Lemme hear it, Marta." I can hear how miserable he feels and the deliberate effort he's spending on applying patience to his tone of voice.

I read. *"Beginning on Friday evening in Duke City and its environs, no vehicle will run, if the person in the driver's seat is legally drunk, that is, with a 0.10 percent of alcohol by volume*

Chapter Three

in his blood. Let time pass and metabolism occur, or substitute a sober driver, and the vehicle will not be affected." Clyde is silent. "You there?" I ask.
"Yeah, I'm here." Clyde sounds very weary.
"I thought maybe you passed out again."
"No. I was listening."
"Well? What do you think?" I ask.
"Think? I don't think anything. It's silly," Clyde says, not very enthusiastically.
"You didn't think the muffler thing was silly. Why is this?"
"I don't know. I don't like it."
"Somebody has figured out how to enforce our DWI laws. I must say I do like it."
"Well, I don't."
"You got caught. Twice. But if you hadn't been, you would have been a hazard on the highway. What about that?"
"I don't know about that."
"Well, I'll let you go. Have a good day at school."
"Yeah," he mumbles. "Thanks, Marta. Thanks a helluva lot." We hang up.

I was working on my next HUNK O' LOGIC -- all about DWI and Mothers Against Drunk Drivers -- when I heard talking in the backyard. More like arguing, maybe. Dad was raising his voice.
"What are the signs for, then?" I hear. And, "So we'll die buried in our own trash?"

I went out and found a policeman watching Dad shovel compost. Dad was not looking at him and the policeman was almost apologetic. "I'm sorry, Sir, but that's the way it works."
"We pass laws -- but we have other laws -- that make it impossible -- to enforce 'em," Dad says, timing between shovelfuls.
"Well, littering is really more a question of education than enforcement, don't you think?" the policeman says, trying hard to be friendly and reasonable.
"I taught school for years -- it'll take centuries that way -- we don't have time."
"Well, I hope you're mistaken, Sir."

Dad straightens up. "If you'da seen that litterer throw his beer can on my place, you'da had the right to stop him, right? Pull him over and study his face, and examine his driver's license, and get his name and address and social security number and be prepared to prosecute him in court as the one who threw the beer can on my place. Right?"

"Well, yes," the policeman admitted.

"And sovereign citizens, like me, do *not* have that right to stop criminals in the act. Correct?"

"Criminal --?"

"Isn't littering a *crime?"* Dad squeals.

"Well, there's a law against it," the policeman tries to explain, "but --"

"But we don't mean it," Dad says, and resumes shoveling.

"I'm sorry you take that attitude, Sir. I mean, we do have to stop littering, but --"

"If you'da seen him do it -- *would* you have stopped him?" Dad asks sharply, still shoveling.

"Uh, maybe. Depending on what was going on, maybe."

"Sounds like maybe-not to me," Dad growls. "Unless maybe you were looking -- for an excuse -- to stop him anyway -- for some other reason."

"Well, now --" Then the policeman stalls.

Dad continues shoveling. "When you go -- maybe you'll be so kind -- as to pick up -- the beer cans and shitty diapers -- they threw on my place last night -- they aren't mine -- I don't want 'em -- and I can't locate the owners -- and I'm gettin' mighty weary -- o' pickin' up after 'em."

Dad shovels without looking up. "Well, I'll be going, Sir," the policeman says, finally. Dad does not reply. "Good day, Ma'am," the policeman says, saluting me smartly as he crosses our back patio and strides up our driveway to the front.

I studied Dad a long time, without going to him. He shoveled in silence. With steady rhythm, he moved a great deal of compost in a surprisingly short time. He is in good shape, physically. But he's disturbed, mentally.

* * *

Chapter Four

Dad was snickering to himself at breakfast several days later. I looked at him expectantly a time or two, and he seemed almost embarrassed. He was trying to get control of himself, without telling me whatever it was that was tickling him.

"You're sure in a good mood this morning," I say, pouring him another cup of tea.

He snorts, and then grins at me. "I been thinkin' of my crazy dream."

"Tell me."

"Well, it's a little crude, for mixed company, y'know -- but it's funny at the same time."

"I'm a big girl. Tell me, so I can enjoy it, too," I urge, glad that he's feeling so good.

He's eager to tell it. "Well, it started with a kind of public announcement. It wasn't a visual picture. This part of the dream was an audio, y'might say."

"Let's hear it."

He quotes in a deep voice of authority. *"Beginning on Monday morning, all litterers will find their penises formed in the shape of the letter 'L'!"*

I almost choke on my tea. "What!?"

"Yeah! That's what it said! And then it got funny. Pictures flashin' by, kinda fast, y'know -- and all funnier'n hell, seemed to me like."

"What pictures?"

"Guys lined up at a public urinal, all pissin' on each other, and jumpin' up and down, each one tryin' to avoid the stream squirtin' sideways from the guy next in line. Then the guys lined up sideways at the urinals, pissin' at right angles, tryin' to learn how to aim it straight, at an angle -- all singin', 'We aim to please!' A guy pointin' his pecker out over the Grand Canyon, and piss gushin' straight up in the air and all over his white shirt and necktie --"

At first I pretend I'm not amused, but then a laugh explodes from me, and the two of us are roaring. "What a weird dream, Dad! You *are* crazy, y'know!"

"I know," he bellows, slapping his knee. "It's hopeless."

I calm down a little. "You seem to think that litterers are your direct responsibility."

"I am mighty tired of pickin' up their shit from my place. And I get plenty disgusted driving downtown in all the crap that blows all over everything there."

"But it's not *your* job to clean it up," I protest. "Or to stop it."

"I know. But I have to clean it up here, on our place. I thought of putting up a sign, 'City Dump,' so people would *quit* throwing their trash here, but then I pictured someone bringin' it by the dump-truckload."

"You take it all too personally. Some people are filthy. We live in the same world with them. We have to make the best of it," I say. Dad grins broadly. "Was that funny?" I ask.

"No. I just thought of another part of the dream. I was in some medical clinic, explaining to the doctor. 'It was an accident! I didn't drop it on purpose!' I'm wailing. He glares at me and says, 'No excuses. See if this splint will fit!'" He bursts into fresh laugh.

"I'm glad you find it funny," I say, not amused nearly as much as before.

"Well, there's a flaw in the idea, anyway," he says.

"I'll say," I agree. "What's *your* flaw?"

"It doesn't punish female litterers."

"So it doesn't. But punishment isn't --" He interrupts with a fresh outburst of giggling. *"Now* what's so funny?"

"Just remembered another scene from the dream. A whore house. The ladies made the customers line up and display their

Chapter Four

equipment. They sent away everybody who had an L-shaped pecker!" He laughs more uproariously. "How could you *do* anything with that -- that disability?"

"There's another flaw in it," I say.

"Tell me," he giggles.

"The punishment doesn't fit the crime. What does litter have to do with -- with *that* idea? You're just being hostile. And, like you said, a little crude." But we both have to snicker further, thinking privately about it.

* * *

Strange things are going on again. Clyde was to pick me up downtown and take me out to lunch. I was standing on the corner, watching all the folks go by.

An overdressed lady, painted unskillfully, in tight skirt, too-high heels and an outlandish sun hat, came wobbling by, chewing on a chocolate candy bar. Just as she reached me, hips swinging in ridiculous fashion, she tossed the candy wrapper to the sidewalk. It stuck to the heel of her shoe. She took several wobbly steps, with the wrapper clinging to her heel. I was afraid the piece of paper was going to trip her. She noticed it, too, and stopped.

She tried to scrape the wrapper off with her other shoe, but had no success. She kicked her foot in annoyance, but the wrapper would not drop.

Finally she lifted her foot and picked the wrapper carefully from her stiletto heel and then primly dropped it in the middle of the sidewalk. When she put her foot down, the wrapper slid across the sidewalk and stuck to her heel again. Static electricity, no doubt.

"Son of a goddam bitch!" the woman shouts. Several people striding by look at her strangely without stopping. The woman kicks and stomps her shoe violently. The heel snaps, but the wrapper clings persistently to her shoe. "What the shit is going on?" the woman yells. "My new shoe!" She glares at me.

"Try the receptacle the city has provided, Lady," I suggest with a sweet smile that seems to make her angrier.

"What in hell are you talking about?" she snarls.

"You're littering," I tell her. "Or trying to." I think of Dad, and smile, knowing this scene would tickle him. But it makes her more furious. She no doubt thinks I'm mocking her.

She picked the wrapper off her shoe and hobbled unevenly, with one heel three inches shorter than the other, to the trash can at the curb. She dropped it in with a final sneer at me and limped away. After several steps she took off both shoes and strode on down Central Avenue barefooted.

* * *

By the time Clyde arrived, he was so late I was not much in the mood for lunch. We ended up at a drive-in. Very formal and romantic -- a hotdog and a canned soda in Clyde's hunk- o'- junk car. Then he drove me back to the office.

At a red light, I was staring straight ahead, holding my 7-up can in my hand. Clyde and I don't have a lot to talk about, really. I was wondering why I bother with him at all, except that I don't quite know how to tell him to get completely lost.

"Finished?" he asks.

"Yes," I say, and then I catch myself. Clyde doesn't read minds, the way Dad sometimes does. "Finished with what?"

"Your can," Clyde says, grinning. "Lemme try a set shot." He's pointing at a trash receptacle on the curb.

"No, I'll hold it."

"C'mon! Lemme try!" So I give him the can. He tosses it at the trash barrel, but his throw is short, and the can strikes the barrel and bounces back into the street and under his car. "Shucks! Missed," Clyde laments.

"You're going to leave it there?" I ask, as Clyde pulls the car ahead.

"Sure. The light changed. Can't block traffic, can I? What the hell?" We hear a clunk-clunk-clunk in the back on the underside of the car. "Now what?"

"You insist on keeping this barely moveable wreck of a car," I say, half-amused and half-annoyed.

Clyde pulls over and gets out. I hear him move something

Chapter Four

metallic. He jumps back in right away. "Nothing serious," he says. "That can was sticking to the tire, and banging on the pavement. I just took it off." He pulls back into the traffic. I can still hear the clunk-clunk-clunk. "That wasn't it. You've got serious problems in your rear-end, I'd say." He pulls over again and gets out. "Look here, Marta. You don't believe me."
I get out and he's pointing at the 7-up can stuck on the right rear tire. "Why is it sticking fast?" I ask. "What holds it there?"
"I don't know, but I don't have a rear-end problem, anyway," he declares, and pulls the can away. He lays it in the gutter and stands up. We hear a metallic scraping sound and when we look, the can is stuck against the tire again. "What the hell!" Clyde explodes.
I reach down and pick up the can. "Here. Let me have it. It's mine, anyway. C'mon, get me back to the office."

* * *

Dad had a story to tell when I arrived home. "Wait'll you hear this, Marta. This is the best yet."
"Best what?" I ask.
"Oh -- uh -- I dunno." He acts as if I caught him at something. "Best HUNK O' LOGIC story for you maybe," he says, recovering his good mood.
"Logic seems to be in trouble these days," I mutter. "Maybe I should look for a new angle."
"Naw, it's perfect," he gloats. "Lemme tell ya."
"O.K. I'll fix tea." I'm feeling much more weary than he is.
"Kid was driving by on a bicycle. Dropped a soda pop can and it bounced funny and he ran over it with his rear wheel and it threw him down. Crash! He got up and looked around and rubbed his shins. Picked up his bike and when he tried to shove off, the wheels didn't turn, and he fell over again.
"'Son-of-a-bitch!' he yelled. I was standing by the road."
"What were you doing there?" I ask.
"Oh -- uh, just -- uh, I dunno," he falters. "It feels like he's

been caught again somehow. "Just studying the traffic patterns, ya might say." I look at him carefully. "Anyway, the kid looked his bike over, and spotted the can. 'Damn,' he growled. It was wedged in tight, between the rear tire and the fender. He had quite a time gettin' it out. Cut his finger. He finally pried it loose and dropped it by that rambling rose bush of ours. He shoved off again, or tried to, but the bike dumped him again!

"'Mother--' he yelled. Well, he yelled more than *that*," Dad says, grinning. "The can was wedged in between the tire and the fender again. He pried it out and threw it as hard as he could across the street. But the damn can sailed like a boomerang -- it was smashed pretty flat by that time -- and came back and landed beside the bike wheel.

"Kid stood the bike up, and the can was resting aginst the tire. He tried to kick it aside, but couldn't. It stuck to his foot, or to the tire.

"'Take the can with you, Sonny, since it's yours anyway. I don't want it,' I said to him. Startled him, I guess. He sure looked scared. Grabbed the can and stuck it in a paper sack he was carryin' and shoved off and rode away without lookin' back."

Dad and I look at each other a long moment. "You seem pleased," I say finally.

"You bet!" he answers. "Littering's gonna be harder to do now."

"What's causing *that?*" I ask.

"Well, how should I know?" Dad says, shrugging his shoulders and raising his hands palms up.

* * *

I found another want ad, but didn't bother Clyde with it. *"Beginning on Monday morning, litter dropped by pedestrians in Duke City will cling to the right foot of the litterer. Litter dropped from vehicles will adhere to the right rear wheel of said vehicle. Citizens are encouraged to use receptacles provided by the city, and the sanitary land-fill provided by the county."*

Debate is now in full swing in Duke City over what is called

Chapter Four

The Influence. It started in our newspaper between the Editor-in-chief in his unsigned column on the editorial page and the ever-more-popular column entitled, HUNK O' LOGIC. The Boss and I don't exactly agree in our attitude toward it -- The Influence, I mean -- but we're selling papers, which pleases him. People are sending in great quantities of letters to the editor, and KTLK is buzzing with it, too.

"Duke City has never been so clean and safe and quiet. It is not at all clear how this has been accomplished, but some power is enforcing laws which we have all agreed we want."
-- HUNK O' LOGIC

"A strange Influence has been unleashed on Duke City. It is not at all clear how it works, but it must be regarded as dangerous. Who, or what, is behind it? Who is in control of it? What will be tampered with next? How will this Influence be combatted, when it is doing something illegal or subversive? The Wielder of the Influence must be apprehended and stopped."
-- Editor of THE DUKE CITY DAILY

"I like it. My husband can't come home drunk. I don't have to put up with his stink and his boorish nastiness. I actually like him, when he's sober." -- Letter to the Editor

"The Influence is a good thing. Our neighborhood is quieter, now that the motorcycle gangs have to have mufflers on their vehicles." -- Letter to the Editor

"Automatic enforcement of laws is unamerican. Part of the game is to have a chance of getting away with something. Enforcement should be left to professionals."
-- Chief of Duke City Police

"Let me share a strange one with all your readers. I was called to the scene of a domestic quarrel. A drunk man struck his wife with a bottle on the side of her head. The bottle broke and cut her badly. The sight of blood sobered him up enough to

stop the fight, but when he tried to drive her to the hospital, his car wouldn't run. The Influence prevents it, you know. The lady bled to death before I could get there. Of course, there's no telling how many people he might have killed, driving her to the hospital, but as it turned out, he's being held now for murder, instead of DWI and involuntary manslaughter."
-- Deputy County Sheriff

"We think the Influence is marvelous. When you find out who the Wielder is and how he does it, please send him to our fair city. We'll put him to good use and pay him well."
-- Mayor of Santa Fe

"The Influence is unfair. I was hauling a load of trash in my pick-up, and a barrel slid off the back. It stuck to my wheel, dragging me off the road and upsetting me in the bar ditch. Damaged my truck and wasted half a day getting all that garbage to the dump."
-- Letter to the Editor

"The Influence is helping me straighten out my marriage, I think. My husband was going to the drug store, he said, but never came back all night. In the morning he was all contrition and apologies. It seems he stopped at the apartment of a new employee at the office. They had a couple of drinks, but when he went to leave, he couldn't get the car to run. She wanted him to stay all night, but he felt remorse and guilt, and spent the night locked in his car. That made her furious, so he tells me. But he says it taught him a lesson."
-- Letter to the Editor

"The Influence has brought joy to our church. Brother Amos, our pastor, was in the church Saturday night, practicing his sermon, and Sister Rachel, the organist, was there, too, practicing the hymns. Brother Amos pulled a quart of Southern Comfort from the back of the bottom drawer of his desk and asked the Sister to join him in celebrating. He confessed that he didn't know exactly *what* they were celebrating, but they celebrated and found out that they liked each other more than they thought. They tried to go home about midnight, but their

Chapter Four

cars wouldn't start. So they went back into the church and found out that they liked each other even more. And they were still there when the congregation began to gather in the morning. He announced to us that they were getting married that same evening, and that he was swearing off Southern Comfort for ever. Praise The Influence, which works in wondrous ways, its marvels to perform!"   -- Brother Malachi

"The Wielder of the Influence must be found. We urge the police to exert every effort to apprehend him. His mind is warped. He has incredible power at his fingertips. If and when he turns it against the so-called good of society and begins to use that power for his own selfish and greedy purposes, he will be hard to stop."   -- Editor of THE DUKE CITY DAILY

"There is no evidence that The Influence, or its Wielder, is in any way dangerous or sinister. It strikes this writer as notable that such remarkable power should be wasted on such minor matters as mufflers and litter. But even so, a cleaner, quieter, safer Duke City is not something to be ungrateful for."
-- HUNK O' LOGIC

* * *

I was kept hopping for a while, keeping track of The Influence, collecting anecdotes, and polling the public unofficially. Then a very unusual letter to the editor arrived. I wanted to publish it in my column, and perhaps react to it, but, no. The Boss hid it among the letters to the editor.

"I am writing to assure all my fellow sovereign citizens that my motives are pure. I am not a dangerous maniac. I have used what you call The Influence only to enforce what we have collectively declared that we want, through the passage of local ordinances. Noise, DWI, litter -- I am assisting all of us in getting rid of these problems.
"Complaints about no exceptions and no extenuating circumstances interest me greatly. No fixed tickets, no acquittals

on a technicality, no bribery at the top or bottom of the system. Instead, automatic enforcement of the law, with the intent of educating and training all citizens. This is done, not by wishing and lamenting, but by the operant conditioning brought about by enforced compliance.

"I have been considering theft, but difficulties come to mind. *'Beginning on Monday all stolen articles will give off an offensive high-pitched whine, which will continue ever louder until the object is restored to its rightful owner.'* That would help with addicts stealing jewelry and TV sets. It would drive fences utterly mad in a short time, and probably put pawnbrokers and professional flea market vendors out of business. But there are problems.

"When is a borrowed unreturned book really stolen? What would be the effect of this on the entire lock, latch and burglar alarm business? I'm in no position to help them retool.

"What about white collar crime? Embezzling, padded expense accounts, false budgets, income tax evasion, and cost overruns, so-called -- what would whine? The data in the computers? And consider the very land mass itself -- in these parts it is all stolen, much of it *twice!* How did the King of Spain obtain the right to give it away? Or the Boss of Texas? You see, I have my problems, too.

"Perhaps you, and the general public, could help me think this one through. Meanwhile, I can only say, 'Trust me.'"

-- The Wielder of the Influence

* * *

I arrived at home one afternoon and found the Animal Control Wagon parked in our driveway. Voices drew me to our backyard. Dad was talking earnestly to two uniformed men. A dead dog lay at the feet of one of them. "What happened?" I ask.

"I shot him," Dad spits out curtly. "Caught him at the rabbits."

"Oh-oh," I murmur, worried. Firearms are illegal inside the county.

But one of the strange men stoops and begins drawing a burlap sack over the body of the dead dog. "Well, we'll be going, Mr. Myers. Sorry about your rabbits."

"Oh, like I say, this wasn't bad," Dad says, almost cheerfully. "At other times, especially in winter, I've arrived too late and found a real mess."

"Call us, if you need us again."

"I sure will," Dad says, and the men drag the dog out the gate and up the driveway.

As soon as they're gone, I turn on Dad. "What're you doing shooting off that gun of yours inside the county?"

"Protectin' my rabbits."

"What did those men tell you?"

"They quoted the firearm ordinance, and then said they didn't blame me, and hauled the dead dog away."

"They didn't give you a hard time, at all?"

"They say the city is covered with stray dogs. I know our neighborhood sure is. Some have owners, and many do not. This one didn't. The men seemed to appreciate the help. We even considered organizing a Sunday morning posse. Keep all humans at home or in church, and sweep through an area, blasting every dog that is out on the streets. But then they figured sentimental publicity would not allow it."

"Did you have to kill this one?"

"It was killing my rabbits."

"How many?"

"Two -- and a wrecked hutch to repair."

We're both silent a moment. "It's too violent," I say, finally.

"I think I agree. The law says a dog must be on its owner's property, or on a leash at all times. I've amended that to say that a dog *is* on its owner's property at all times and thereby claim as mine every dog in my fenced-in back yard. I guess I can kill my own dog if I want to, just like I could my own pig. There wasn't time for much else."

"Time?"

"Once a dog gets to the blood, he'll go through the whole rabbit herd, killing everything. He turns into something almost human." Dad tries to grin, but I'm not seeing anything funny.

"I've come out, like I said, especially in winter, and found everything dead. Blood all over the snow and hutches torn all to hell. I resolved a long time ago to stop it, no matter what the laws may say."

"How'd it get in here?" I ask.

"Jumped the fence, from the top of that shed, I think," he says, pointing to a low little building on Clyde's side of the fence. "I checked for tracks, waiting for those men to get here. I guess Clyde left *his* gate open."

* * *

I decided I needed to get away from everything -- Dad, Duke City, Clyde, and the HUNK 'O LOGIC column. I drove to Jemez Springs, a resort up in the mountains, and checked in. It felt good to be alone, and the hot mineral soak was marvelous. I stayed several days, enjoying the fact that no one around me knew who I was or expected anything of me. I guess that's what a vacation is supposed to do.

On the evening of the second day I was in one of the few public eating places in the village and couldn't avoid hearing conversations around me. Loggers and their girl friends, and a few visiting hot springs tourists like me, and the bartender and the Indian waitress -- it was all one big noisy conversation.

"How in hell are we supposed to cut logs without equipment? This isn't the goddam Middle Ages, for Christ sake!"

"What equipment?"

"A chain saw, f'r instance. I'm not gonna chew 'em down, like a goddam beaver!"

"What's the matter with your chain saw?"

"There isn't a chain saw workin' within six miles o' here. Every camp's shut down, for lack o' chain saws. And most o' the goddam trucks. Guys are already moving over to San Gregorio. At least their equipment works."

"You mean every chain saw in Jemez Springs is shut down?"

"Every goddam one. And most o' the trucks. And my kid's trailbike."

"Y'know, something like that was going on down in Duke

Chapter Four

City, I heard."

"Yeah, I heard that, too. Cars and motorcycles and semis won't go unless your muffler muffles."

"Who the hell ever heard of a muffler on a chain saw?"

"Might not be a bad idea. Jemez Springs is pretty noisy."

"Bullshit. It's a lotta bullshit."

I listened without saying anything. It did seem that the muffler Influence had invaded Jemez Springs. Logging around the village was at a standstill, at any rate.

When I returned to Duke City, I went straight to the office. I was going through the mail, when the Boss called me in and told me the muffler Influence seemed to be no longer in effect in Duke City. Wanted me to check it out.

I called the Chief of Police. "Well, it was gone for a few days, there, but now it's back," he tells me.

"Back?"

"It's working again, but not quite in the same places."

"Tell me what you mean."

"We've noted carefully the places where traffic jams occur as unmuffled traffic enters Duke City. In fact we gave your paper that list, so you'd let the general public know."

"Yes, I remember seeing it."

"But now we're in the process of making a new list, 'cause the locations are different."

"And you said it was gone for a while. Exactly when?"

"I'm not sure we noticed it right away. The bike boys in San Rafael Park caught on, though, and by evening, they had their baffles back out. We ticketed some of 'em, but couldn't catch 'em all."

"When was this?"

"Let's see -- two, no, three nights ago. But it came back this morning. New traffic jams -- but in different locations, like I told you. It's like it moved. Went away, and then came back to a different place."

"Would you call your new list of locations to me, as soon as it's ready, please?" I ask him.

"Sure. Maybe together we can figure it out."

I worked a while at my desk. When the secretary brought me

the new list, I asked for a copy of the old one, and packed it all up and took it home.

I found Dad in the back patio in the middle of a mess. He was cleaning the garage. Sweeping, scrubbing and going through everything. "What brought this on?" I ask him.

"Well, it needed a good cleanin' out," he says.

"You look worried about something," I tell him. "What's the matter?"

"Oh, nothin'," he replies and dumps a coffee can of rusty nails on the patio floor and begins fingering them and putting back the straight ones.

"Want any help?" I offer.

"No, I'll do it," he mutters. Something is the matter with him. Worse than ever, I decide. I shouldn't have gone away and left him.

I'm marking the traffic jam locations on a city street map on the kitchen table when Clyde comes over. "I missed you," he says. "You never said you were leaving." He means it as a reproach, but I don't react.

"I took a much-needed vacaton," I say primly and go back to my map.

"Whatcha doin'?" he asks.

"Marking the locations of the muffler Influence."

"Oh, let me see!" he exclaims. I have almost all the original list marked with red X's. I add the last two while Clyde watches. "They're all in a circle," he says.

I look at it, and see the circle immediately. I marvel that I hadn't seen it before, but the eyes do that. Or the brain. It's as plain as can be now. "Yes, I see it, too. Thanks! Let me draw it."

I run for a compass from Dad's desk. It takes some experimenting to find the center. "Further west," Clyde says. "Bigger radius. Just a little bigger. Further south. There!" I draw a circle that intersects with every X. "Look at the center!" Clyde yelps.

I look at the hole the compass has made in the map. "What about it?" I ask.

"The location of it!" Clyde sings. "It's right here!"

Chapter Four

I stare. The hole is on Isidro Boulevard, very near here, if not right here. "What does that mean?" I ask in a whisper.

"I don't know," Clyde says. "Sure seems strange, though."

"I have another bunch of X's to draw," I say, feeling strange. Not exactly scared, but -- peculiar. "Want to help?"

"Sure."

I read off the second list, and Clyde marks a new set of X's in green. "It's another circle," I say, when we're about half-way through the list.

"Yes." Clyde has become serious, too. We draw the second circle. The center is on the other side of the river. Downtown somewhere. What would move it over there? I look at the new hole in the map. The exact location is the newspaper office building.

Something flashes in my memory --

I took a garbage bag full of junk mail and plastic packaging out to the garage. We have to lock it up, to keep it away from stray dogs, even inside a fenced-in yard. I plunked the bag down on the others and turned, and my eye caught something. Up on a shelf, where I never look and have no business really -- the garage is Dad's territory, with bee stuff, rabbit pelts, seeds, tools, jars of screws and that kind of thing. I spotted something -- one of Dad's little black plastic pyramids, just like the ones I moved from the kitchen table some while ago.

I picked it up and studied it, hefting it in my hand and turning it over. Nothing to it. Pressed plastic pyramid, square base, four triangular sides. On the bottom of the base a piece of masking tape was stuck with the numeral "2" written on it in pencil. On impulse, I put it in the pocket of my apron, and went back to the house.

Later, when I was changing clothes, I held the pyramid in my hand again. I wondered if I was imagining the tingling I thought I felt in my palm, as it sat there. And the ringing in my ears when I held it close -- was that whine already in my head, or was the pyramid causing it? Was it vibrating? I put it in my purse and forgot about it -- until now.

I jump up, startling Clyde. "What the hell --?"

I grab my purse and dump its contents on the table. The

gesture reminds me of Dad dumping the can of rusty nails. Some of the contents embarrass Clyde a little, but I'm too excited to care much. I mean women carry things -- but I don't care. I rummage through it all and find the pyramid. It's been in my purse since -- when? Before I went to Jemez Springs -- I jump for the telephone and dial. "Let me talk to the Chief of Police." Clyde is staring at me, wide-eyed. "Chief? Marta. Yes. Listen, uh -- any late-breaking information on the current location of the muffler Influence? ... It's moved again! ... Where to? ... Uh-huh. I see. Well, I'll let you know if I find out anything. Or figure out anything." I hang up and stare past Clyde for a minute.

"Marta, I think maybe sometimes you're as crazy as Mr. Myers," he says softly. "Why'n hell'd you dump your purse?"

I step past him to the kitchen door and look out. Dad's cleaning the garage. He's looking for this pyramid. Because this pyramid controls the location of the muffler Influence. The Chief just told me -- it's moved back to where it was at first.

I say nothing to Clyde. I worry more than ever about Dad. He's crazy and he's in trouble. And he's, maybe, dangerous.

* * *

Chapter Five

Dad was missing when I got up for early breakfast. But his pick-up was gone, too, so I didn't worry much. At least he wasn't up to his old vanishing trick, or whatever. But where would he go so early?

I scanned the morning paper. Same horrible national and international news. HUNK O' LOGIC -- more Influence anecdotes, with only a few typos. Want ads -- I've been watching them, and found a new one, of the weird kind we've been having lately.

"On Monday morning all stray dogs in Duke City will assemble at the Animal Control Shelter. Keep your dog at home, inside a fenced-in yard that keeps it in, or on a leash. If your dog is missing, you may ransom it at the Shelter."

I sat thinking. Dad is gone, and today is Monday. He's doing something with his crazy pyramids. But what? And how? And how much trouble is he in?

He's been untalkative lately, not much fun to be around, and evasive when I ask him things. Should I turn him in? For what? Who would believe me? Do I want to anyway? Has he done anything wrong? What is really going on? Am I going crazy? Is he crazy? Or is he something else? Something worse?

I don't know how long I sat there. A good while, for sure. Dad did not return. At mid-morning, I called Clyde. His summer school is over. "Want to go for a ride with me?" I ask.

"Sure, Marta. Be delighted."

I drove across town, toward the Animal Control Shelter.

Clyde talked all the way.

"I tell you, Marta, Mr. Myers has gone stark raving bananas. Yesterday I was walking home from the meat market, in front o' your place there, and little old lady Bernal was asking him, 'Have you seen my Fifi?'

"'No, I haven't, thank the Powers That Be.' He was really nasty.

"'Well, I never!' she wailed.

"'Never learned to keep that goddam worthless poodle at home!' he barked, scowling at her something fierce. 'Comes over here and takes her dump. Goes over to the neighbors and drives all their dogs crazy, waking up sovereign citizens at four in the goddam morning. No, I haven't seen your Fifi.' He was downright mean. Mrs. Bernal began walking away from him, and he followed her. 'But don't be surprised if she strays for good one o' these days,' he sneered.

"'What do you mean by that, you awful man!' She was wailing, and near tears.

"'When Fifi doesn't come home, you can try looking for her at the Animal Control Shelter.'

"'Oh!' she yelped. 'Have you seen the dogcatchers around here?'

"'We won't be needing them anymore,' he said. Now what the hell could he have meant by that remark, Marta?"

"I'm not sure," I admit. "Look!" We were on an overpass across the freeway. The Animal Control Shelter lay in the distance, snuggled in the cloverleaf. Traffic had us stopped, and no vehicles were moving on the freeway itself below.

"What's going on!" Clyde yelps.

"Dogs!" I cry. "The Stray Dogs of Duke City!"

The Shelter was overrun with dogs. They covered the freeway and pressed on the chain link fence between the freeway and the shelter. Others were trotting across the overpass, going around the stopped traffic.

"What's the matter with them?" Clyde asks.

"They are not on their owners' property, and not on a leash," I intone, quoting the want-ad, and the law.

"No, I mean, look at them! They're not -- not normal."

Chapter Five

I look more carefully. They're marching forward, almost unseeing, not hurried, not hesitating, tails extended out behind them, heads up, ears cocked as if listening. Moving. Going where? Toward whatever's attracting them.
I open the door. "What're you doing?" Clyde wails.
"I'm going down to the Shelter. You coming?"
"No way. They scare hell outa me."
"I figured as much. Stay with the car. I'll be back."
"You're crazy, Marta!" he wails again.
"I know. It's hopeless," I mutter. I got out and walked with the dogs across the overpass and down the long curving ramp which led to the shelter entrance. Soon the dogs were packed so thick they couldn't, or didn't, proceed. Each one had a little territory, it seemed. I could proceed among them, and did.

Hundreds of dogs, of all breeds, all sizes, all colors. Boxers, pit-bulls, German shepherds, collies, poodles -- could that one be Fifi? -- basset hounds, bloodhounds, greyhounds, dachshunds, weimareiners, pomeranians, dobermans, great danes, chihuahuas, samoyets -- and all the possible and impossible crosses and combinations. Pampered house and lap dogs, tough scavenger dump dogs, wild mountain pack dogs, south valley killers of livestock -- all standing around, as if waiting for the meeting or the concert to begin. Or, rather, as if it had already begun and they were paying attention to it. Listening to something, they were. They ignored me.

I found the superintendent of the shelter in tears. His state of mind shook me out of my own stupor. I may be going crazy, but that guy was already gone.

"Good day, Sir," I begin. "I'm from the DUKE CITY DAILY." I show him my press card.

"What am I gonna do?" he whimpers. "People abandon their pets here at the Shelter, especially on week-ends. But look at the poor dears! I can't feed 'em all. I don't have cages for that many. What'll I do?"

"Sir," I say, "The city will obviously have to take strong and drastic measures. Tell me, did you have any idea there were this many strays in Duke City?"

He doesn't hear me. "The poor things. And they're thirsty.

When did they eat or drink last, I wonder. And they need loving!" He kneels down and embraces the mean-looking chow at his knees. The dog ignores him. It is busy listening to something.

I work my way back to the car. Clyde is in a panic. I turn the car around carefully, and inch my way out of the ever-enlarging crowd of dogs. It takes hours. Clyde is no help. The sight of the dog-congregation has affected him, turning him into a blubbering child. I decide never to bother him again and hope he doesn't bother me.

Dad still isn't home. What am I doing to do with him? When I find him...

* * *

Dad's totally non-committal when he comes in, mid-afternoon. "Where have you been?" I demand. I sound shrill and shrewish, more than I intend.

"Been?" he echoes, calmly. "Delivered a worm bed early. Came back to load another about mid-morning. Where were you?"

"Clyde and I went to the Animal Control Shelter," I answer.

He grins slightly. "You did? What'd you find there?"

"A very large number of stray dogs, that's what!" I retort. After staring into his face, I confront him. "What do you know about it, Dad?"

"About what?" He looks as innocent as a lamb.

"About the assembling of the stray dogs of Duke City at the Animal Control Shelter!"

"How would I know anything about it? I was busy doing my own business -- selling worm beds."

I couldn't get anything more out of him. "I see you cleaned up the garage. Looks nice."

"Yeah, thanks. It was a mess."

"Did you find what you were looking for?"

"Who said I was looking for anything?" he retorts, maybe too quickly.

"Oh, I don't know. That's what occurred to me as I watched

Chapter Five 135

you working."
 He did not respond, and I let it rest. The evening news showed pictures of the huge dog assembly near the shelter. Also, an interview with the Mayor, who suspected, at that time, that the whole thing was being greatly exaggerated by the media. His comments were cleverly juxtaposed by the news editor, showing on split screen the Mayor's pooh-poohing comments and at the same time the massive congregation of dogs. Dad and I both laughed. Other pictures showed the shelter superintendent in tears.
 Next morning Dad was gone again when I got up for breakfast. I went to the office. About mid-morning the secretary called me to the window. "Look, Marta."
 We stared down at the concrete canyons of downtown Duke City. Traffic was stalled. Horns were blaring. The streets and sidewalks were covered with dogs, moving sedately, almost as if on parade, going around vehicles, pedestrians, litter barrels, poles -- relentlessly marching. "Where did they come from?" the secretary asks.
 "I don't know. The Animal Control Shelter, probably," I reply.
 "You mean they let them *loose!*" she wails.
 I glare at her. She sounds like the mad superintendent, except his madness is compassion, and hers is fear and ignorance. "Where are they going? That's what I want to know," I say and trot to the elevator.
 I joined the dog parade, letting them guide me. We turned a corner here, then turned the other way there, zigzagging, but never hesitating. They were hearing something and following it. I stayed with them, and they did not object, or notice me, or each other, at all.
 After several blocks, they stopped marching, bunched up solid in a crowd. I worked my way forward among them, and turned one more corner, and saw where they were heading. City Hall. The big marble building was surrounded by dogs. The wide stairways on all sides, the streets on all sides, the flower beds, the fountain -- all covered with dogs, standing, waiting, listening. I turned back.

It was a little more disconcerting walking against the flow among the dogs, seeing their muzzles head-on, and their entranced concentration. And all their amazing variety -- huge dogs, little dogs, brown dogs, black dogs, white dogs, spotted dogs, striped dogs, brindle dogs, shaggy dogs, bald dogs, old dogs, puppy dogs, injured dogs, healthy dogs. Pedigreed, crossed, mongrelized, mutts, curs and pooches of every kind.

Finally I reached the office parking lot. I got in my car and drove carefully, inching along. The dogs gave room and went around, and I moved slowly enough so as not to bump them. I drove toward the Animal Control Shelter. About half-way there, the crowd of dogs thinned out. At the Shelter itself, all was calm, or so it appeared, until I found the superintendent.

He was in a very bad state. "They left! They went away, early this morning. Who will take care of them? They'll starve! They'll be run over in the traffic!"

"But you said you couldn't take care of them!" I remind him. "And you couldn't. There are thousands of them!"

"But who else will look after them?"

"What made them go?" I ask.

"I don't know," he laments.

"Try to remember what happened this morning," I say. "Maybe we can figure it out."

"Nothing unusual. Several people came, early, looking for their lost dogs. But there were too many! Then suddenly, they turned that way and marched away!" He waved toward downtown.

I could get nothing more out of him. I drove toward the office, and then decided to avoid the mess. The mayor doesn't need *me* to figure out what to do about media hype.

I drove to San Rafael Park, over on the west side. The bike boys were lounging, but I didn't approach them. Manny waved. I parked at an empty table and got out and sat. I have to decide what to do about Dad. His pyramids have something to do -- something *impossible* to do -- with all this mess. I'm afraid to confront him, or it. He's really a dear old man. He's really not mean or dangerous. But the Influence, whatever it is, may be dangerous, and he's tangled up in it. But he's not a kid.

Chapter Five

He can take responsibility for his actions -- he always taught that everybody should do that.

I heard the bike boys laughing, and looked up. Several dogs were romping near the motorcycles. I watched. One was a bitch in heat. Four not-quite-exhausted males were entertaining her, taking turns. Manny and the others hooted loudly, from time to time, especially when the bitch changed partners. The dogs were quite intent on what they were doing, even though the males were becoming exhausted.

As one finished, he loped away, toward me. I saw him freeze suddenly, then raise his ears and tail. He listened a moment, and then started marching away from me and the bitch and the other dogs, heading east in a straight line. I watched him until he disappeared over the ditch bank.

When I turned back to the other dogs, another male had already heard whatever it was that summoned the first one. Standing in that same place, about halfway between Manny's table and mine, he stood, ears up, tail up -- and then away he marched. The other dogs were still busy with copulation. But as each male finished and drifted in my direction, he was caught up in some kind of summons, and with renewed vigor hied himself off downtown.

The bitch let them go. She lay down and licked herself and seemed appreciative of the respite.

* * *

Government in Duke City came to a standstill. City and county bureaus remained closed. Judges dismissed jury panels and adjourned their courtrooms.

City Council met with the Mayor in emergency session. Contingency funds were voted to feed the dogs. Traffic was forbidden in the downtown area.

We put out a skeleton paper. HUNK O' LOGIC was dedicated to further public debate on the latest attack by the Wielder of the Influence.

"What is the source of this power? How does it work? What

will he try next? He must be apprehended and locked away for good, before he further disrupts life in our fair city."
-- Editor of THE DUKE CITY DAILY

I interviewed officialdom and quoted them all. "All the dog excrement that used to be scattered all over the parks and lawns and sidewalks of our fair city is now concentrated on the pavements of the downtown area. It is quite impressive. A new ordinance concerning dog ownership is under consideration by the Council." -- a member of the City Council

"A perfectly adequate law governing stray dogs is already on the books, requiring a fenced-in yard that keeps the dog in, or a leash. We simply underestimated how many dogs there are and how widespread are the violations."
-- Department of Animal Control

"I must say it's a clever trick by somebody to squeeze something non-pentagonal out of the Federal Budget. But it won't work. Everyone knows there are no stray dogs in this country."
-- United States Attorney General, vacationing in Duke City

"The maniac who thought it was macho to drive his car through the dog-assembly at fifty miles an hour, killing ten and injuring several dozen, must be found and prosecuted. It was little better than murder. Could he be found guilty of hit-and-run? Or perhaps, more likely, tax evasion? It is remarkable how many sick people are out loose in this town, and how powerless the police are to control their behavior."
-- Letter to the Editor

I found another want ad. *"The stray dogs of Duke City were moved from the Animal Control Shelter to City Hall because of the Mayor's flippant attitude. It is not yet clear that he grasps the seriousness of the situation. A permanent solution to the stray dog problem must be found. Unfunny jokes from the current federal administration have become intolerable, and will*

Chapter Five

cause the dogs to be moved to the Federal Building."
 The ad didn't say when. I thought the tone was different. Not a simple statement of how it would be, beginning at such-and-such a time. Instead, an inclination to argue, to answer jokes, to punish, to threaten -- and I thought of Dad again. He has something to do with this. What? How?
 I could get nothing out of him. He's meditating more than ever, it seems to me. He shovels more and more compost. And he delivers worm beds early mornings. But he talks little. That child-like playfulness is gone. He's worried about something.
 "Dad, are you in some kind of trouble?"
 "What kind of trouble could I be in?"
 "I don't know. That's why I'm asking. Something is upsetting you."
 "I thought something was upsetting *you!*" he retorts.
 "Well, it is. But I think it's you."
 "You want me to move out?"
 I'm stunned. "Move out? Whatever for?"
 "I dunno," he says, looking down. "Something is bothering you."
 "Dad, this is *your* place. I haven't forgotten that. It's just that if you're in some difficulty, and if I can help, I'd be glad to."
 "I'm fine," he growls. "Just fine." And he gets up and goes out and crawls under his worm bed pyramid and closes his eyes.
 I follow him, and watch him. He sits a very long while in the lotus position. When he pops his eyes open, I speak immediately. "Tell me, Dad. Does that thing have any effect?"
 He turns his head slowly to confront me. "What thing?"
 "That pyramid of yours." I touch it gingerly.
 He unwinds himself and crawls out. "I'm not sure," he says, more animated. "I'm sellin' 'em so fast, I haven't had a chance to study the size of 'em scientifically. Maybe it affects the rate at which I sell 'em." He winks and we both laugh and feel a little better.
 But that afternoon I decide it's my civic duty to talk to the Mayor. From his office up high in City Hall we look down on the gathering of dogs below. A dump truck is unloading the evening feeding of dry dog chow beside the fountain. The dogs

circulate in orderly fashion within their congregation, taking turns feeding and drinking. We're too high to smell the results of their digestive processes.

"Something must be done to remove them soon," the Mayor admits to me. "I must confess I didn't take this seriously at first. We had other problems, you know. For a while I thought it was a ploy to influence budget considerations. And then I guess I was hoping they'd just go away, the way they came."

"They may move to the Federal Building," I tell him.

"Why would they do that?"

"I'm not sure. But I'm convinced it's another instance of the Influence."

"That Influence of yours in nonsense, Marta."

"It can't be entirely. Mufflers, DWI, litter -- and now stray dogs. Someone is enforcing, and dramatizing, laws that the City Council has passed and no one has enforced."

"It's silly."

"I think you'll have to get beyond simply repeating that," I say.

"What do you know about this Influence?"

"Very little. I've kept track of the debate, more than you have, I think. I definitely do not believe it is merely silly. Something is going on. The dogs are down there." I nod to the window. "They moved to here from the Animal Control Shelter. And someone claims to be controlling them. That person now threatens to move them to the Federal Building. That will keep downtown paralyzed, but will dramatize that someone is in charge of them. Somehow."

The Mayor looks at me quizzically. "Where'd you get the Federal Building idea?"

"The Wielder of the Influence has stated it in a want-ad. He has never struck without warning. It's his fifth want-ad, that I know of."

"The police will have to monitor the want-ad desk at your paper," states the Mayor.

"Good idea. But meanwhile, I must show you something else." I pull the muffler pyramid from my purse.

"What's that?"

Chapter Five 141

"I'm convinced that this little thing determines the location of a circle, inside which the muffler Influence takes effect. I have moved that Influence -- all the way to Jemez Springs and back -- just by moving this pyramid."
"You can't be serious."
"I am. Leave it here in your desk overnight, and call the Chief in the morning, and he'll tell you that the muffler Influence has changed. The center will have moved from my home to here."
He reaches for it and I hand it to him. "I'm having trouble believing any of this," he mutters.
"I can imagine. I think there may be another pyramid, like that one, hidden in this building most likely, which attracts the dogs. I suspect it was moved from the Animal Control Shelter the day the dogs all came here."
"Where'd it come from? How does it work?"
"I have no idea."
"It's crazy, Marta," he says, fingering the pyramid in his hand. "But I need to do something about that mess down there."
"Yes," I agree. "You sure do."

* * *

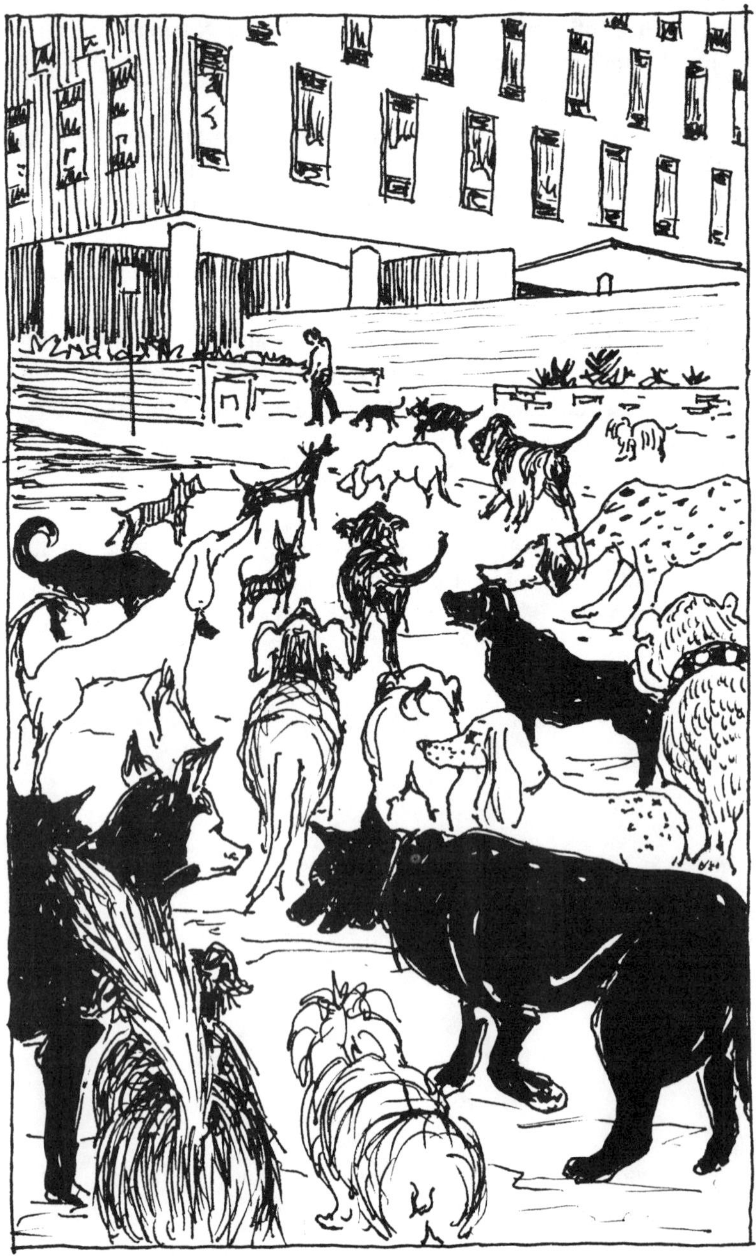

Chapter Six

Dad didn't come home for supper. I sat at the kitchen table, staring at the uneaten meal, feeling half-sick with worry. He's in trouble, I think to myself. He never misses supper without calling. Because of me, he's in trouble.
The phone rings. I grab it and yell, "Hello, Dad?"
It isn't Dad. "Marta, this is the Chief. Your plan worked!"
"What plan?"
"We caught him!" the Chief says, excited. I'm silent. I didn't have a plan. "You there, Marta?"
"Yes," I say softly. "Is he all right?"
"Who?"
"The Wielder of the Influence."
"Sure, he's all right. Locked up safe and sound."
"I'll be right over."
"You want to interview him -- tonight?"
"I sure do."
"You reporters never rest, do you?"
"I'll be right over," I repeat, and hang up.
All the way downtown, I'm worried sick. Hand cuffs, beatings with flashlights, homosexual rapes, murders in prison cells -- all the horror stories I ever heard race through my mind as I cross the river.
I have to walk a dozen blocks to the police detention facility. That's the new fancy phrase for jail. It's part of City Hall, surrounded now by dogs. Some of them are inside, filling the hallways of the new marble building. It's a foul-smelling mess, unless you like the smell of essence of dog.

143

The Chief is feeling good about his catch. "We got him, Marta. And it was your idea!"

"Who is he?" I ask.

"Oh, I don't know his name. Doesn't matter much, does it? They're booking him over at the desk."

"Can I see him?"

"Later."

"Does the Mayor know?"

"He sure does, and wanted you informed right away. It was your story -- you deserve it, he said."

"I wish he'd come down here tonight."

"He's still in his office," the Chief says. "But lemme tell you how we caught him."

"Yes, tell me. But I want to talk to him right away."

"Sure. We started with your notion that there was another little black plastic pyramid, and that someone would try to move it from here to the Federal Building. I posted men on the streets, between the two buildings, on all the different routes a person could take. Instructed 'em to watch for pedestrians and for any change in the dogs, and to radio in right away. I was at the Federal Building, at the main entrance.

"Nothing all afternoon. Not very many people on the streets. Too many dogs. Too much dog shit on the pavement." He grins, and licks his lips. "You understand."

"Yes." I am very calm.

"You don't seem very excited," he notes.

"I'm worried about who it is," I admit.

"It doesn't matter. We got him. Anyway, about seven o'clock, the first call comes in. 'Dogs have turned and are facing in a different direction.' Three calls like that. Then, 'Dogs are following an elderly male pedestrian.'

"'Dogs headed south on Fifth, following an elderly male pedestrian.' I asked for the exact location of the pedestrian.

"'Fifth and Copper.' 'Fifth and Central.' 'Sixth and Central. Dogs changed direction and following.'

"'Pedestrian stopped. Dogs stopped. Dogs are facing the pedestrian from all directions.'

"'Pedestrian moving south on Sixth Street.'

Chapter Six

"I picked two good men and we waited out on the corner of Sixth and Gold. I could see him. He looked worried. He stopped several times and looked around. He studied me from half a block away. Then he seemed to decide something and headed straight for me. As he came within three steps of where I stood on the corner, I made my move.
"'You're under arrest!'
"'You gotta be kidding!' he sneered.
"'Hands up!' I yelled.
"'Whatever for?' he answered, and tried to step past me. I pulled my sidearm on him.
"'Stop right there! Hands up!' I barked at him.
"'As a sovereign citizen I demand to know why I am being stopped, and threatened. And stop pointing that gun at me!' he said, all dignified.
"My men grabbed him from behind and locked each elbow. One of them had handcuffs on him in a second. He slumped to the pavement, went limp, y'know, like a peace protestor. My men held him up, but he wouldn't stand. 'Search him,' I ordered.
"They went through his pockets. The usual things -- wallet, keys, red handkerchief, pen, comb, coins. And this."
I stare at the Chief. He's holding up between his fingers a little black plastic pyramid, just like the one I gave the Mayor. I reach for it and the Chief hands it to me. When I take it, I hear a commotion in the hallway, as police guards scuffle with dogs which are crowding the hall.
I turn the pyramid over. On the bottom is a piece of masking tape, with the numeral "5" written in pencil.
"He refused absolutely to co-operate. Wouldn't talk. Wouldn't give his name. Wouldn't tell us what that thing is, or is for, or does, or anything. Wouldn't walk. We had to drag him. They're having trouble booking him, I hear, because he will not speak. Won't say a word."
"May I talk to him, now?" I ask.
"He won't talk to anyone," the Chief answers. His phone rings. He picks it up. "Yes, Sir. Yes, she's here. Wants to talk to him. O.K., we can try. But he's not --" He hangs up.

"Mayor wants us up in his office," he says to me.

* * *

The Chief and I hadn't sat down yet in the Mayor's office when two young police officers dragged an old man through the doorway. It was Dad, completely limp. I ran to him.

"Dad! What's the matter? Can't you walk? Are you hurt?" I turn and glare at the Chief.

"He's all right. He just won't stand, or talk," the Chief explains patiently.

"We can't book him, Sir, according to procedures, because he won't talk. We read him his rights, and all that, but he just glares at us." The men are holding him by the armpits.

"Dad! Tell me you're all right," I plead. Dad smiles grimly at me, but says nothing.

"Why are you calling him, 'Dad,'?" the Mayor asks me.

"He *is* my -- my Dad." I turn to him and yell, "Now look at all the trouble we're all in! I hope you're happy!" Dad grins feebly, but still doesn't speak.

"You'll have to get him to talk, Marta," the Mayor says. "He isn't a mute, is he?"

"No, he isn't a mute. He's a stubborn old man!" I glare at Dad. Then I can't help myself, and reach and touch his arm gently. "Are you all right? Not injured?" The young policemen are holding him so that his legs dangle a little above the floor.

His voice startles all of us. "I absolutely refuse to stand or talk while handcuffed."

The Chief laughs. "We handcuff *all* suspects. Does he think he's someone special?"

"He often refers to himself as a sovereign citizen," I say softly.

"Take them off him," the Mayor orders.

"Sir! I object!" yelps the Chief. "He may be dangerous."

"There are five of us, three of you fully armed. Keep your eye on him. He doesn't appear dangerous. Not in the handcuff sense."

Chapter Six 147

"It's against all procedures, Sir," says one of the young policemen. "He isn't even booked properly yet."

"I want to talk to him," states the Mayor.

"Me, too," I add.

The men glare all around. "O.K., over my objection, Sir," the Chief says. "Unlock 'em," he orders his men.

A minute later, Dad is sitting on one of the cushioned chairs, facing the Mayor across his desk. "Now, what's this 'Influence'?" the Mayor demands.

"That word for it came from the debate in the papers," Dad says, a little evasively.

"What's *your* name for it?" the Mayor asks.

"Uh, I don't really have one," Dad admits.

"So -- what the hell *is* it? How does it work? How do we shut it *off?"* the Chief barks loudly, interrogating a prisoner. Dad ignores him.

The Mayor picks up the pyramid from his desk. "When you were stopped, you had this in your pocket. The dogs were following you at the time. We have experimented with it a little, and find that it attracts the dogs, no matter who has it. What is this? How does it work?"

"It attracts all dogs that are legally strays within four miles. By moving the pyramid, you move the attraction. The -- uh, Influence."

"How does it work?"

"I don't think I can explain it exactly," Dad says. "I don't really understand fully how it works myself. Vibrations have to do with it."

"Where'd you get it?"

"I -- uh, activated it," Dad says quietly.

"Why?"

"To get the stray dogs off my property and out of my neighborhood. Shooting was too violent, Marta said, and I agreed."

We all stare at him. "How did you activate it, Dad?" I ask finally.

"I was taught a ritual."

"Well, *de-*activate it!" the Chief yells. "You're interfering with law enforcement!"

"Enforcing laws that you pretend aren't on the books," Dad says to the Chief.

"I want you to shut this thing off," the Mayor says to Dad.

"I can't," Dad confesses. "It's an irreversible process."

"And that other pyramid? The one I found in the garage? It *does* control the muffler influence, doesn't it?" I ask.

"Yes," Dad says.

"You activated it, too?" asks the Mayor.

"That's right," says Dad. He sounds weary.

"And there are two more, aren't there?" I say. "One for DWI and one for litter."

"Right."

"Where are they?" the Mayor asks.

"At home."

"I want them brought here at once," the Mayor says to the Chief.

"Yes, Sir. We'll conduct a search --"

"Wait," I interrupt. "Please. Let me." I turn to Dad. "Where are they, Dad? I'll go fetch them." I turn back to the Chief. "It'll be easier than wrecking our house, and quicker."

The Chief shrugs at the Mayor. The Mayor asks Dad, "Where are they, Mr. -- uh, Mr. --?"

"Bill Myers," Dad says with great dignity. "Sovereign citizen."

"Mr. Myers," repeats the Mayor. "Tell us, Mr. Myers, where the other pyramids are. A squad car will take Marta there and she'll bring them here."

Dad turns to me. "When one turned up missing, I had to be more cautious. Remember that loose brick in the cellar wall, behind the shelves where we keep our home canned stuff?" I nod. "Behind that brick," he said, sounding relieved.

"Let's go right away," I say to the Chief. I turn to the Mayor. "But I still want to talk to him, tonight."

"We'll be right here, Marta," the Mayor says smiling grimly. "Sorry this turned out this way."

"Me, too," I mutter as I make my way out. The young policemen have to wrestle with a pair of dogs who try to enter

Chapter Six

as soon as the door is opened.

* * *

When I returned, the Mayor was in secret emergency session with the City Council in council chambers. The young policemen in the hall were expecting me. I handed over two more black pyramids, marked #3 and #4, and one of the officers took them into the meeting to the Mayor. The other directed me to a plain bare room behind the police booking office. Dad seemed glad to see me.

"You found 'em all right?" he asks.

"Sure. The Mayor has 'em by now. How are you?"

We sit in straight wooden chairs facing each other. "I'm O.K.," he says. "Feel kinda stupid, really --" He hesitates. "Shoulda been more careful --"

"But you're not hurt," I say.

"Not really. Just -- well, it feels like I blew it."

"Yes, it does. Suppose you tell me all about it. Blew *what?*"

"You're not gonna believe it," he says, sounding very tired.

"Maybe not. But I want to hear it."

He looked away. "I don't know what to start with." Then he turned back to me. "I guess it started in Mind Games. I told you one night that I talked to Sol."

"Yes. The Sun. I took it that you were losing your grip on reality."

"I knew you wouldn't believe me."

"Tell me, anyway. What did Sol say?"

"You have answered the first question." Dad uses a deep heavy voice, as if to imitate Sol, I suppose.

"And that question is --"

"What do you want?"

"And your answer was --"

"'Peace and quiet.' I told you some of this already."

"Yes. But I didn't pay very much attention, except to worry about your mental state. Strange disappearances on your part bothered me more."

"Sol taught me The Ritual," he says. I wait. "The Ritual

that activates the pyramids. I had eight of 'em."

"Eight," I repeat.

"Sol did something to 'em first -- but then I have to specify conditions with a separate ritual for each one." Dad doesn't seem to be caring now whether I fully believe him or understand him. He's just getting rid of a heavy load.

"There was a light came down from Sol, up in the corner of my room, down into my eyes and through my body, and down and out of the palms of my hands --" He's holding his hands out, palms down, and moving them in a little double circle round and round. "-- and down into the pyramids.

"Then Sol says, *'You have these opportunities to alter conditions. Be very careful. Define precisely the conditions that you intend to prevail in each case. Define the radius of the circle within which the new conditions will prevail. Write these determinations as precisely as your faulty language will allow. There will be no later deleting or amending. Remember your answer to the first big question.'"*

I'm staring at him. "Dad, how does this work?"

"I asked Sol that. *'You would not understand a correct explanation.'* Then he added, *'Do you understand how a television receptor, or a computer, or a politician's mind works?'* I had to admit not really. *'The pyramid works by controlling vibrations which determine manifestation.'* Sol said. Sometimes I think I almost understand that, and most times I know I don't. It doesn't matter."

"Doesn't matter?" I repeat softly.

"It works anyway, I mean."

"You can alter conditions. Fix new conditions. Dad --" I can hardly speak. "How did you decide *what* to do? *What* to try? What to alter?"

"It's pretty tricky," he says.

"Dogs, litter, *mufflers!* For God's sake, why waste that power? That opportunity!"

"You mean why didn't I make everybody's loose change pile up at my front door? Or transfer fifty dollars from everybody's bank account to mine? Get rich so we can afford to move away from all the noise and filth and commotion and interference?"

Chapter Six

He had thought of the greedy route. "It didn't seem fair, somehow," he continues. "And it didn't seem to have anything to do with 'Peace and Quiet.' I felt like I had to stick close to that, I guess. I tried to do my homework. Found out the details of the laws. Decided to go into enforcement." He grins feebly.

"That's what has the Police Chief mad," he adds. "Can you imagine, so many muffler violations it causes traffic jams when we enforce it? And so many DWI violations, the accident rate is cut in half when we enforce it? And all the hundreds of stray dogs?" He shook his head. "Law enforcement -- but it may finally keep me out of trouble. I haven't *broken* any laws at all, I don't think." He's thoughtful again. "But I blew it. It's really tricky."

* * *

I glared at Dad for a long time. He *is* crazy. But he has access to strange power, too. Frightening power. My mind raced. What might he have done? What could he yet do? He looks like a defeated and bewildered old geezer at the moment. Suddenly something occurs to me. "Dad!"

He's startled. "What!"

"I know of four of those pyramids. Numbered two to five. There are four more?"

"Yes," he says, sounding very weary.

"What happened to number one?"

"I wasted it."

"Doing what?"

"It's a long story."

"I'm surprised the Mayor, or the Chief, haven't asked you already."

"They did."

"Well, I want to hear about it, too."

"It's not interesting. I wasted it."

"On what?" I ask, insisting.

"On truth."

"You wasted it on truth."

"I now believe that that was my closest call with greed. Increase *my* powers, or something. I'm glad it didn't work. But it cost me one." He shifted in his chair. "'Course, right at the moment I'm not interested in activating any more, anyway."

"So there are three more. Does the Mayor know that?"

"No. I deviated from the truth, by evasion and omission. He thinks the dog thing was my last shot."

"Tell me about truth," I urge him. "The truth pyramid, I mean."

"I set it up so that within five feet of it, the truth, the whole truth and nothing *but* the truth is revealed."

"Like my second glass of wine? Truth serum?"

"In a way. I thought I could catch persons lying. Be deceived less. *Know more.* It seemed like a good idea, at the time, but it didn't work."

"What happened?"

"Things look strange -- vibrating, giving off energy somehow. Living things are almost painful to look at. But the sound was the worst. I could hear all the vibrations. Whines and buzzes and resonating booms and woof-woofs and beeps and peep-peeps -- all jumbled together, all at once, too many signals. It was totally unintelligible. Drive a body nuts."

"You *have* been a little -- uh, strange, Dad."

"I know. This thing didn't help any. It was too much. The net was gone."

"What net?"

"The screen we stick up in front of our brains to look at the world through, to listen through. I remembered an old fairy tale about the guy who could hear what other people were thinking. One on one was O.K., and sometimes to his advantage. In crowds, he went mad -- too many signals."

"So you wasted one. What'd you do with it?"

"It made me cautious. I've been afraid to set one up on stealing. It would reach too far, mess up everything. Dishonesty lies at the root of our system, I'm afraid. So, I turned to law enforcement."

"Where is the first pyramid now?"

"In our chicken pen."

Chapter Six 153

I have to laugh. "So Clyde *did* hear you, talking to the chickens?"

"Maybe so. I can hear it when I gather eggs. Just a little momentary reminder. And they love it." He chuckles softly.

"What's funny?"

"Chickens are supposed to be stupid. But they can handle truth better than us brilliant humans."

A policeman opened the door and summoned both of us to the emergency session of the City Council.

* * *

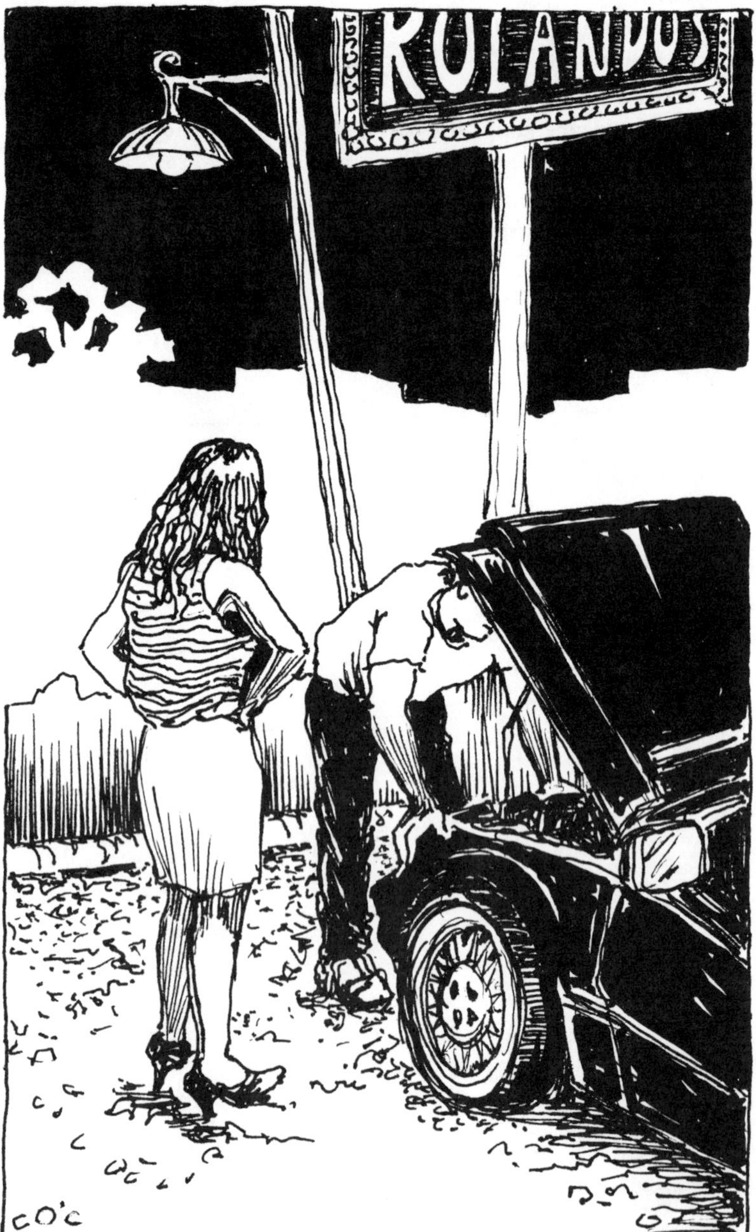
ROLANDOS
cO'c

Chapter Seven

"Ladies and Gentlemen, I didn't expect this meeting to turn into a debate," the Mayor says to the Council. "Please interrupt me, if I convey incorrectly to Mr. Myers the consensus of the group." He's being a little sarcastic, it seems to me.

He turns to Dad. "Mr. Myers, you are aware that you have disrupted life in our city in a manner which is unacceptable. However, no one on the Council can determine exactly what crime you're guilty of. Some have proposed 'impersonating an officer,' but that would probably not hold up in court. Your want-ad warnings, which finally enabled us to catch you, demonstrate that you were not conspiring secretly or acting out of malice aforethought."

"They demonstrate his civic pride and concern," a councilwoman interposes.

"Exactly," the Mayor continues. "Therefore, we are planning at the moment to release you into the custody of your daughter, on a kind of unofficial probation." I smile and sigh audibly.

"What about the pyramids?" Dad asks.

"The City is confiscating them, Mr. Myers. Part of your probation, we could say."

"I don't object. But I'm curious what you're going to do with them," Dad says with a faint smile.

"That was most of our debate. The Council has decided that the dogs must be led back to the Shelter immediately, and then dispersed or eliminated, as rapidly as possible. Fines will be imposed strictly as owners are identified, and quadrupled for repeat offenders. A modern city really is no place for a loose dog."

"That's what I thought," Dad mumbles.

"The other pyramids will be kept here, temporarily, downstairs in the main lobby in a display case under twenty-four-hour police guard. The Council, if I read the consensus correctly, is for the most part grateful to you, Mr. Myers, for your assistance in enforcing the laws on noise abatement, drunk driving and littering. Many members are prepared simply to leave the pyramids in place, and put warning notices on the outskirts of town where each Influence takes effect. They suggest widening the roads at those points, to allow drunks and unmuffled vehicles to pull over. We're sorry you didn't make them all effective at the same distance, which would've made that plan less expensive.

"But other council members have persuaded us that the general public must make the final decision. Therefore, a special referendum will be held two weeks from now, in which all citizens will be encouraged to vote on each of the four influences.

"Mr. Myers, we will try to keep your name and picture out of the papers. Some individuals have had bizarre experiences because of what you've done. Accidents with litter, for example, and missed job interviews because of stalled vehicles, that sort of thing -- and we fear that they may want to punish you directly. My advice is for you to lay low until after the referendum."

"What if they vote, 'No'?" Dad asks.

"In that case, we'll take the pyramids by plane two hundred miles beyond the two hundred mile limit, off California, and dump them, encased in concrete, into the ocean."

* * *

A policeman led Dad down to the booking room, to pick up the contents of his pockets, minus one pyramid. The Mayor escorted me back to his office. "He's a remarkable gentleman, Marta. I wish he would have consulted with me before he activated those things."

I have to grin. "Oh, you have ideas of your own about

Chapter Seven

altering conditions?"

"I sure do," he agrees, grinning back.

"Like, *'Beginning on Monday evening, all City Council members will agree with me,'*" I intone.

"Ha! Hadn't thought of that! No, I was imagining help in solving problems we're getting nowhere with. Your father picked on things we thought we had solved already."

"Maybe that's because you think laws alone constitute solutions."

"No doubt. I had no idea, I'll admit, that there are still that many stray dogs loose."

"Or that so many cars entering Duke City are in violation of one thing or another. Enforcement creates traffic jams."

"That's right," he says, grinning again.

"What problems do you have in mind, that you could use help with?"

"Air pollution. It's a mess, and we can't get at it. The inspection program has been declared illegal by the Supreme Court, as you know. We're losing federal funds, because the air is so filthy. And I don't doubt for a minute that the health of all of us is in jeopardy."

"I'm not sure Dad could help much."

"Why not? We'd figure out something. *'Vehicles that pollute the air beyond so many parts per million will not run.'*" he intones. "Looks downright easy to me."

"Yes, but Dad thinks his pyramids should be limited to what he calls 'peace and quiet.'"

"Well, wouldn't it be quieter and more peaceful -- City Council meetings certainly would be -- if we weren't destroying the air here in Duke City, not to mention our lungs?"

"I'm not sure Dad would see it."

"It's a form of littering!" the Mayor insists.

I smile. "Maybe you should talk to Dad about it."

"Another thing." The Mayor really wants to talk. "Something dangerous and serious that the media aren't on to yet. Talk about your peace and quiet --" He stalls.

"What is it?"

"This town is criss-crossed every day by trains and semitrucks and tank trucks, carrying all kinds of deadly material. I mean *lethal!* We catch a tiny percentage of it. And what do we do? Escort 'em right on through. We don't want the stuff in our landfills. We want it away from here. But someday there's going to be some kind of mishap, and you can forget about peace and quiet."

A knock sounds at the door and the policeman is back with Dad in tow.

* * *

When we finally arrive home with both vehicles, I sit Dad down at the kitchen table and rewarm his midnight supper. I let him finish it while I hold in all the pressure that's seething inside of me. When he says for the umpteenth time, "I blew it," I explode.

"You sure did!" I bark sharply.

He eyes me over the rim of his teacup. "You're really angry, aren't you?"

"I am, indeed!"

"I just couldn't think of all the different little side-effects. The way it ramifies in all directions, how *serious* it really is --"

"What a big job it is, being God Almighty!" I bellow.

"It amounts to that, kind of."

"Alter conditions!" I yell. "Who are *you* to alter conditions?"

"Well, Sol said I had answered --"

"You should have *declined* the privelege," I interrupt. "On the grounds that you're not sufficiently deified, not omniscient enough, not -- something."

"Sol warned me."

"But you went ahead anyway!"

"Funny old stories went rattling in my head, after Sol said something about modesty and caution. Modesty, and he didn't mean nudity --"

"Nudity!" I'm fuming, and Dad's almost talking to himself.

"No, no, he meant be careful. A modest scope. I remember stories. The Fisherman's Wife, who wanted everything. Finally wanted to be God --" He grins feebly. "God Herself."

Chapter Seven

I am not amused. *"You* want to be God!"

"Not really. In fact, the whole thing has scared hell outa me."

"I sure hope so," I growl.

"The Monkey's Paw -- wishes that turn into horrors, and you have to waste the wishes on each other, cancelling 'em all out, one after another. A kid who wanted an unlimited supply of porridge -- and it bubbles up out of the pan and off the stove, and fills up the kitchen and out the door and down the street and engulfs the whole town."

I'm staring at him. "You want to be God, and then you waste it on mufflers and dogs."

"Picking what to do was the hardest thing of all. What would *you* have done?" he asks.

"The Mayor has some ideas."

"You told him I have three more?"

"No. I just listened. He may call you, however."

"What does he want to do?"

"Something about the polluted air in Duke City. Some of us can remember when it was *clean*. Transportation of toxic waste, of different kinds -- he didn't say exactly."

"And what do you suggest?"

"My god, the nuclear thing comes to my mind immediately! *'Beginning on Tuesday morning, no nuclear reaction will occur within ten thousand miles of Duke City.'*" I'm screaming. "I mean, we have *huge* problems, as a species, and as a community. And you're wasting it on mufflers! I can't believe it!"

"I have a three hundred mile limit," Dad says, as serious as I've ever seen him. "I thought about nuclear, but didn't know how to handle it. And I didn't want the CIA and the Pentagon on my ass."

"Think about it some more," I say, trying to control my exasperation.

"I will. I'm sorry to have caused you so much worry and trouble, Marta. I really didn't intend any harm to anybody. Your sympathy for that dog I shot got to me -- I wasn't feeling any of that at the time. I was thinking of dead rabbits -- oh, I dunno. Maybe it's too complicated. I don't wanta be God.

Even though he does seem to be in need of assistance. And if He isn't a She."

"Don't blame God. Humans are at the root of the problems. Maybe you should work on the humans. All the unhappiness in the world -- inside the Pentagon, even -- all the selfishness and greed and lying. All the miserable people."

"So far I never get anywhere thinking down *that* track," Dad says very seriously. "Automatic enforcement of happiness -- I've tried to figure it out."

"Well, try some more."

"O.K., Marta. I will." He stands up. "But now I'm going to bed. G'night."

* * *

Chapter Eight

Now he's disappeared again. He was in his room. I saw him there, meditating at his desk, but when I came out of the bathroom, he was gone. Nowhere in his room. Not in the house anywhere. Not in the garden. Not shoveling compost. Not at the wood pile. Not at the meat market.

He's been quiet lately -- subdued, you might say, while the city debates The Influence. I wish I could ignore it in my HUNK O' LOGIC column, but I can't altogether. I mean, the whole town is buzzing with it. But I have to be careful, not to call attention to myself or Dad. Mostly I'm just quoting the opinion letters that come in.

But where is Dad? He could go for a walk, I suppose, without telling me. I become angry every time I think about how he's wasted his powers. And now that I know about them, his disappearance feels like another of his tricks. I've caught myself calling, "Dad? You there? Dad!" Talking to myself in his empty study. Could he make himself invisible? Have I heard, or just imagined that I heard, his soft chuckle, while I'm looking for him?

* * *

Clyde called. "Marta, you gotta come see this, in the back yard."

"I'll be right over." I haven't been bothered with Clyde, since the day the dog thing started, but I consent immediately, without thinking.

"Look here!" he calls, as I step through the gate in the fence between the two back yards.

"What is it? My God --" I see a strange kind of mark, a line drawn in the dirt, and across the paving stone walk between his back door and the little low shed by our fence. A long slightly curving arc -- "What is it?"

"Look!"

I bend closer. The line is composed of living things. Ants and cockroaches, mostly, but other crawly things, too. "I never saw anything so weird," I murmur. "They're -- where'd they come from?"

"I don't know," Clyde says. "Sure funny, isn't it? What caught my eye was a mouse --"

"Mouse!"

"Yeah. Scampered across the yard and then -- well, it was kinda like it bumped into something and bounced off. It scrambled along, trying to cross that -- that *line* there. But it couldn't. It went along sideways, jumping up and falling back, and scooting and hurrying -- you know how they do. All along the line, clear out the back under the lace vine there --" He points at his back fence covered under thick green vines. "It couldn't cross the line. And these things can't either!" He points at the arc at our feet.

I look again. The roaches and ants and bugs and rolypoly things are all trying to cross an invisible line, but they cannot. They are held back. They rear up a little in the air, and then topple. The line is the jumble of their crawling bodies. They can't climb over and they can't dig under. Their numbers are increasing, too, it seems to me.

"Let's follow it," I suggest. Out back it curves and cuts under the vine fence. We turn back toward Clyde's house.

"Look in here," he calls from inside his kitchen door. The line continues across the kitchen floor -- mostly tiny little ants, the kind that ruin sugar.

"Let's look out front." We go out his front door and cross the yard. The line curves toward our place and then goes along the edge of Isidro Boulevard in front of our house. As I watch, a stray cat scoots across the street in traffic. It has safely

Chapter Eight

dodged the oncoming cars, when it bumps into something I don't see and bounces back into the path of a car, which runs over it. "Oh!" I scream, and run. The car goes on, oblivious. The cat is dead. Ninth life, snuffed out.

"That's what happened to the mouse out back!" Clyde yells. "I mean, no car ran over it, but it couldn't cross this line."

"Clyde, I gotta find Dad."

"Mr. Myers? What's he got to do with it?"

"I don't know. Something, you can bet." I started toward our house, and Clyde followed.

* * *

He was sitting at his desk. "Where have you been?" I shriek.

"Been? Right here. What's the matter, Marta?"

"A car just ran over a cat out front --" Clyde begins.

"You're up to something!" I yell at Dad. "Another of your tricks!"

"Ahh --" He stalls briefly. "How can you tell?" He stands up and licks his lips in embarrassment.

"You're admitting it! Come out here and look!" I pull him by the arm.

We go out into Clyde's back yard and study the living line. A mouse hops out from under the lace vine in the back, scrambling against the invisible barrier. Then it sees us and turns back and scampers out of sight.

"I'll be damned," Dad says, scratching his head. He kneels to study the line. He reaches and stirs the writhing insects with a finger.

"Don't touch them!" I yell. "Filthy cucarachas --"

"I had no idea there'd be so many of them," he muses. "Oh-oh -- I wonder." He stands and marches back into our yard.

Clyde is staring at him speechless. I follow Dad, and Clyde tags along. Now he'll be in on our secret, I think. Our secret little problem.

Dad drives a pitchfork into one of his compost piles and lifts a forkful, turns it over and studies carefully. "I feared it.

Shoulda thought of that."

"Thought of what, Mr. Myers?" Clyde asks, almost in awe.

"No roaches, no rolypolies, maybe no microbes even, in my compost. And it won't work without 'em. Shoulda thought of it."

"What are you talking about? What have you done?" I scream. "Activated another one, right?"

"Yes," he admits.

"One what?" Clyde asks.

Dad and I are ignoring Clyde, except that I'm vaguely troubled by my feeling that a serious secret is getting out where I don't want it. But I can't stop the process.

Dad sits dejected in the back patio. "I tried *de*-fense." He accents the first syllable. "Sixty-five feet. Now you gotta admit that's modest," he says to me.

"De-fense," I repeat, with his accent.

"Yeah. *'Beginning this morning --'"* He's imitating the tone of his want ads. *"'-- intruders will be excluded. Thieves, trespassers, strays, scorpions, centipedes, black widow spiders, cockroaches, ants, flies, mosquitoes, disease-carrying microbes. Within sixty-five feet.'"* He looks at me, defeated. "But now I've ruined my compost process."

"And killed a cat," I add.

"I did not kill a cat," Dad says wearily.

"You altered conditions," I accuse. "Playing God again."

"I was trying to make life better for you --" He stalls. "For you -- here, on this place."

"Me?" I ask, genuinely puzzled. "Don't blame this on *me!"*

But he's deeply concerned. "I blew it again, looks like," he mumbles.

"Maybe you can move it," I suggest. "Or throw it in the ocean."

Dad looks at me sadly. "I blow it every time."

"Move what?" Clyde asks, bewildered.

"Where is it?" I demand of Dad.

"In my desk."

"Go get it. We'll watch the line in Clyde's yard," I say, getting up.

Chapter Eight

Clyde and I go into his yard, while Dad goes into the house. In a few moments we see the line move. The insects scramble more frantically than ever, as the line forces them back. At one point they cannot get away from between the invisible pressure and a block wall. They are crushed to a brown pulp. "Don't walk so fast!" I yell at Dad, who is ambling toward the gate.
"What's happening?"
"You're crushing them!"
"Is that bad?" Dad calls, but he turns and goes back into the house.
Clyde and I look at each other. "What the hell is going on, Marta?" he cries. "I *know* he's loco, but I think maybe we're *all* going crazy! Is it catching?"
"I'm not quite sure," I mutter.
We go back and find Dad sitting in the patio. "It's impossible," he's mumbling. "I try to think of everything, but I cannot. I can't foresee all the ramifications."
"That's why you're not God," I say, not nastily. Now I'm feeling sorry for him.
"I'm trying for peace and quiet. Keep intruders out. No breaking and entering at our place. No plague, either, I think, while we're at it. But what intruders did I forget?" He eyes Clyde carefully, almost as if he notices for the first time that Clyde is hearing all this. "I actually thought of you, young fella, but then decided that that was not my affair."
"Dad!" I yelp.
"But it was modest," he continued. "Seemed like it couldn't hurt anybody, or anything. I mean, the mice can just hole up someplace else. But, no. Trouble right away. A dead cat that I'm not really mad at, weirdness in your back yard, compost process shut down -- it's hopeless."
"Maybe you should quit, then," I suggest.
"Sure looks like it," he admits.

* * *

I'm assembling the high points of the debate that's going on all over Duke City. The referendum is tomorrow. Man-in-the-street interviews dominate TV news. KTLK airs a continual discussion. At the paper we're having a hard time deciding which to print of the dozens of letters to the editor. People who meet at gas stations and supermarkets and convenience stores all over town talk about The Influence with total strangers.

"We should know who it is so we can honor him."

"Citizen of the Year."

"Crimestopper Extraordinary!"

"The city needed help enforcing its own laws. Until now these laws were unenforceable and therefore meaningless. We call in with complaints of one kind or another and are told, 'We have this law, but we can't, or won't, be doing anything about it.' Now something is being done."

"Law and Order Forever!"

"Private citizens have no business enforcing the law."

"Every citizen has a constitutional right to try and get away with it."

"At last the law really is no respector of persons. The law of littering is now just like the law of gravity."

"'Permanent solution' is a Nazi phrase. And how else will the city permanently solve the stray dog problem now, except by turning the Animal Control Shelter into an Extermination Camp? Auschwitz on the Rio Grande!"

"He's a dangerous sorcerer and should be burned at the stake."

"It's a marvelous advance in technology. Isn't science wonderful?"

"The changed auto accident rate qualifies him for the National Safety Award."

"The Nobel Peace and Quiet Prize..."

"Criminal of the Year. I'll kill him when I find out who he is."

"I wish he would activate one that combats theft. We'd find out how much of our economy *is* theft. Just think -- no more burglary, no more petty pilfery, no more shoplifting, no more embezzling, no more cost overruns, no more tax evasions. It would bring business and industry to a grinding halt."

"Drunkenness is a sin which God will punish. We don't need

Chapter Eight

a special automatic mechanical influence to punish it."

"When laws are enforced automatically there is no freedom, no room left for man's exercise of the freedom to disobey. Man no longer needs correction, or punishment or exhortation."

"Jesus died on the cross so our sins could be forgiven. The Influence prevents our sinning. If it isn't stopped, Jesus will have died in vain."

The Mayor appeared on TV. "I want to talk to you all about tomorrow's special referendum on The Influence. I refer to the automatic enforcement of noise abatement, D-W-I, littering and stray dog laws.

"I am convinced that the person who set all this in motion is not a dangerous criminal, nor a mad scientist, nor a visitor from Outer Space. He is one of us, an ordinary citizen of our community. I like him and believe he can be trusted. I am not yet ready to reveal his identity, but I wanted you to know my feelings about him.

"He tells me he has been concerned for a long time about what he calls 'interference.' Noise, theft, litter, dogs and traffic careening out of control -- these problems threatened continually the peace and quiet of his home. He became aware of our difficulty in enforcing the laws we have regulating these things.

"He stumbled upon a strange power. He does not understand it and I do not understand it. The Physics Department and the Psychology Department of the University are studying it, but their spokesmen are not as yet very hopeful of understanding it in the near future. Their long-held theories don't account for this new power in any way.

"However, that doesn't matter. While they adapt theories, we as a community have some decisions to make. The center of each of the four influences is a modest little black plastic pyramid. Three of them are on display in a shatterproof case here at City Hall. You are invited to come see them. The fourth one, which summons stray dogs, is at the Animal Control Shelter. I want the dogs to assemble *there,* not here.

"The pyramids appear to be indestructible. We have not been able to crush them or burn them. It's part of the mystery of the strange power.

"So we have to decide what to do with them. The people elect the City Council, which passes laws. The people also elect the Mayor, who enforces laws. The Influence is so strong, and so uninterested in exceptions and deceptions, that we are giving this decision back to the sovereign people. What do you as a community want? Enforcement, with the help of The Influence, or removal of The Influence, leaving us with the old situation -- unenforceable laws on the books, while we kill ourselves with noise, litter and vehicles out of control? Perhaps you can tell, I as a private citizen will be voting for The Influence. But I want *you* all to decide. Those who choose not to vote are voting with the majority. Good evening." A weary smile flitted across the Mayor's face as the image faded from the screen.

* * *

Dad came into the living room in time to catch most of the Mayor's speech. He sat down in an easy chair and flopped back, looking more relaxed than I've seen him in a long time. When the ads resumed at the end of the speech, I turned the TV off. Dad remained reclined back, his hands folded over his belly, fingers interlocked.

"You're looking better," I say cheerfully.

"Feelin' good!" he says, grinning broadly.

"Now what's up?" I ask, suspiciously.

"Up? Nothin'."

"You're up to something," I accuse.

"Naw." He looks around the room, as if checking things over. "Just talked to Sol again, is all," he says, trying to sound off-handed about it, but not succeeding.

"Oh-oh. More trouble."

"No such thing." He says no more, and continues looking around, concentrating on the flowers in my blue vase, the philodendron hanging in the corner and the paintings on the wall.

"So what did Sol say?" I ask finally.

"I kept muttering that I blew it."

"Well, you did."

"Sol doesn't think so. *'Not too badly,'* he said. *'You asked*

Chapter Eight

for nothing for yourself, which is a pleasant change for me from previous encounters with humans.' I mentioned my peace and quiet thing. Sol said, *'You try to change people. You can't. We can't. Not by force. Remember your own story of the ant farm.'"* Dad stopped.

"What ant farm?" I ask.

"In history classes, I used to illustrate my viewpoint about miracle stories in the Bible, with the story of the little boy who had an ant farm. Moses and the Israelites at the Red Sea. Big miracle story -- God saves the Israelites and zaps the Egyptians. God is the boy, and the world is his ant farm."

"I don't see any ant farm in the Moses story," I say.

"The ants do their thing. The ants go marching two by two. They build tunnels, eat, copulate, lay eggs, fight -- whatever ants do. Every once in a while the little boy reaches over the edge of the ant farm with a stick -- I'm gonna get that ant -- and pokes the ant farm with his stick. Kills the ant. Tears up tunnels. Interferes! But the world isn't like that. If there *is* a God, she doesn't interfere like that."

"Oh," I say, taking it all in.

"Sol said, *'That's what you've been trying to do. But you can't change people that way. You may kill a few, but it doesn't change anything.'"*

We're silent. We can hear traffic shushing on the street out front. The surf of the sea of humanity.

"I wondered, to Sol, if the last two pyramids were any good," Dad continues.

"'They're perfectly good. You haven't activated them yet.'

"'I'm afraid to,' I said.

"'Good,' Sol said.

"'Maybe I shouldn't,' I said.

"'No "should" to it. No hurry either.'

"'I'm tempted to influence the referendum,' I said.

"'Resist that,' Sol said, almost like giving orders. *'Let the community decide what it wants. Sovereignty of the people, and all that. Another of your pet ideas.'"*

We're silent again a long time. "Anything else?" I ask finally.

"Yeah. It was a little strange. I asked, 'How long are these things good for?'

"'Long?' he answered. *'You fix the radius of the circle in which you want it to work --'*

"'No,' I said. 'I mean how much time?'

"'*Time. Time. Yes, I almost forgot. You have time. Let's say a very, very long time.*'"

I stare into Dad's face. He looks younger and fresher and more able to do whatever he might want to do than people my age, and younger. "How old *are* you, Dad?" I whisper.

"Old enough to know better," he says, grinning.

"You're not going to tell me?" He's silent. "And where do you disappear to, from time to time? Don't tell me that you don't."

"Don't ask me, Marta," he says, very seriously.

"What kind of power do you have?"

"It isn't mine. I am unworthy of it. I haven't used it very well. And I'm not important. But don't ask me."

"Are you all right? I shouldn't worry about you?"

"I'm fine. Don't fret, please, even if you can't find me for a long time. Time is very strange." He's silent again, and I wait. "Just one more thing," he says after a while.

"What's that?"

"I love you very much. And I don't want to cause you any trouble at all. I hope you know that."

"Sure, I know that."

"Good," he says. He doesn't say any more.

I finally get up and say, "G'night, Dad. I love you, too. But sometimes I can't help worrying." He smiles but doesn't say anything. I go to bed, wondering what kind of man I'm living with.

* * *

Chapter Nine

Disappeared again. It's been several days. I finally gave his name to Missing Persons. But no luck, and I didn't really expect any. I don't think he's dead. He planned it. It's another of his tricks. I wish he could have trusted me enough to tell me what he's up to.

Maybe he's not up to anything. He hinted that he was going away, when he said he activated pyramid number six for me, to defend me and our place here. As if he wasn't going to be around. And he told me he loved me, last time we talked.

He left the last two pyramids where I can't miss them, on the mantel above the fire place. They glow in the dark like little night lights. Number Seven and Number Eight. I don't know if they've been activated or not.

I miss him. Strange feeling -- I ache for him. I know it's silly. We never thought of each other as lovers. I mean, he's my Dad! *Old!* A very peculiar old man, I'll admit. And yet that's how I miss him, partly. Not just to talk to. To *be with.* To be close to. I must be as crazy as he is.

Strange car wreck out front the night before last. I was in bed and the crash woke me up. I don't think it was really that loud, either. A car was turning into our driveway and bumped into something. I heard the cardoor open. When I went out, I found a man with a revolver in his hand, lying unconscious beside the car.

I ran in and called the police. They took the man in and had the car towed away. Chief came over next morning to tell me that the car was stolen and the man was a dangerous escaped convict. "Sure lucky we caught him," the Chief says.

"Dad caught him," I say.

"He did! Where is he, anyway?"

"Missing."

"If he's missing, how did he catch that felon?"

"Never mind," I say. More questions led to my filing the missing persons report next day.

So I sit here, thankful for the defense pyramid, staring at the last two on the mantlepiece, mooning over Dad as if we were passionate lovers, and wondering what he's experimenting with and where. And expecting him back, too, somehow --

And I try to imagine what I would do with the power to alter conditions. Evidently I think bigger than Dad, for one thing. I think nuclear. Peace in the world. Psychopathocrats governing huge empires. But I hear a question in the back of my mind. "Can a world that keeps needing to be saved be worth saving?" Where do world leaders come from anyway?

I think of overpopulation. *"Human females under twenty and over thirty-five will be sterile."* Or, *"Human females will give birth only once."* China is trying that, without Dad.

"Rapists will be inflicted with such intense testicular pain that rape will be unconsummated and the rapist permanently reconditioned."

Poverty --

Unhappiness --

Kindness, hopefulness, love -- I think I understand that no one can legislate that kind of thing. There is no automatic enforcement, of those things. But I must admit it's tempting.

Alter conditions -- it would be a mess.

Clyde just called. I told him to come over. He's such a harmless jerk. And it's not fair to compare him to Dad. I have to chuckle, to think Dad considered excluding Clyde, as an intruder. That would have been funny to watch. Dad's been looking out for me all along. But where is he?

* * *

More Fine Southwest Books

from AMADOR PUBLISHERS:

CROSSWINDS
A Darkly Comic Modern Western
by Michael A. Thomas
ISBN: 0-938513-02-8 [169 pp. $8]

A young construction worker with low impulse control struggles to be a sane hard-working citizen, exposing the duplicities of modern society, which crush all that is unique and genuine from the old rural values.

Michael Thomas was born in Raton and reared in Alamogordo, New Mexico, near ground zero of the world's first atom bomb blast. His ambition to become a surfer was difficult to achieve in New Mexico. Today he is an anthropologist, counselor and teacher.

"Novels set in Eastern New Mexico are rare...really good ones even more so! The droll languages reaches into our unrecognized prejudices and false fronts and drags them jolting into the light of a marijuana bonfire. A superb writer has found his way onto the list of a budding New Mexico publisher. Both are to be congratulated."   -- BOOKTALK

"Very funny, very convincing novel of the Great Southwest, with accurate and nicely-drawn characters. It would make a good movie, though I'd hate to lose the dry, Ring Lardner-style narration."   -- ALBUQUERQUE JOURNAL MAGAZINE

"The book exudes the Southwestern ambience, celebrating the land, the people and the language. The characters include several strong women, red-necks, ex-hippies, wetbacks and fundamentalists. The undercurrents of meaning beneath the surface of this joyful and amusing story are notable."   -- THE RATON RANGE

"This blue-collar novel is concerned with current moral problems such as ecology and racial discrimination."   -- BOOKS OF THE SOUTHWEST

"CROSSWINDS reminds me of so many people I know. For all his craziness the hero has a sensitivity to people and the environment. He is a real New Mexican, and I haven't seen this character in literature before. He's from 'the other New Mexico.'"   -- Denise Chavez, author of THE LAST MENU GIRLS

"...a big marijuana stash, put-upon wetback laborers, a batch of ornery people and sundry 'shenanigans, complications and stratagems'...the development of the narrator from a foul-mouthed adolescent into a worthwhile human being..."   -- NEW MEXICO MAGAZINE

CAESAR OF SANTA FE
A Novel from History
by Tim MacCurdy
ISBN: 0-938513-07-9 [240 pp. $11.95]

This rousing tale describes the administration of Governor Luís de Rosas, in colonial New Mexico around 1640. A tempestuous love affair determines, temporarily, the outcome of a bitter struggle for power between government officials and Catholic missionary/clergy.

Tim MacCurdy is a literary historian and critic. He has published fifteen books of criticism, while teaching Spanish language and literature for 32 years at the University of New Mexico. This story is well-researched; to understand this period, one can molder in the archives, or enjoy this novel.

PRIZE-WINNER! Best First Novel, 1991 -- WESTERN WRITERS OF AMERICA

"Tim MacCurdy combines an intimate knowledge of New Mexico history and a story teller's still in this remarkable novel. It should become one of our classics."
-- Tony Hillerman, author of A THIEF OF TIME

"...the product of impeccable research... Seventeenth century Santa Fe springs fully to life... leaves the reader with the feeling that he, too, was there." -- THE TEXAS REVIEW

"New Mexico's mountains, deserts and isolated communities, reeking with old Spanish tradition and Indian folklore... MacCurdy displays a keen intelligence and sense of irony... an astute observer of the vagaries of human character... superstition, ignorance, power struggle, cruelty, violence... wry humor suffused with tragedy and pity. MacCurdy delights in and delights us with the often raucous life of early New Mexico." -- THE SANTA FE NEW MEXICAN

"Santa Fe of 1640, with whipping post and Inn of the Humpbacked Cat, comes to lusty, brawling life in this story of conflict between Governor Luís de Rosas and the priests who were nearly all, according to MacCurdy, engaged in exploiting and alienating the Indians. Rosas falls in love with a married woman, which exacerbates the hostility between peninsular Spaniards and <u>criollos</u>. Excellent detail and believable people." -- BOOKS OF THE SOUTHWEST

"The novel is quick and entertaining reading, giving insight into the clandestine activities of Governor Luís de Rosas and his cronies, whose exploits are chronicled in existing judicial and ecclesiastical records from that period... packed full of liaisons, class consciousness, witchcraft, warfare and a varied cast of characters." -- NEW MEXICO MAGAZINE

Retail Price: $4.00 each

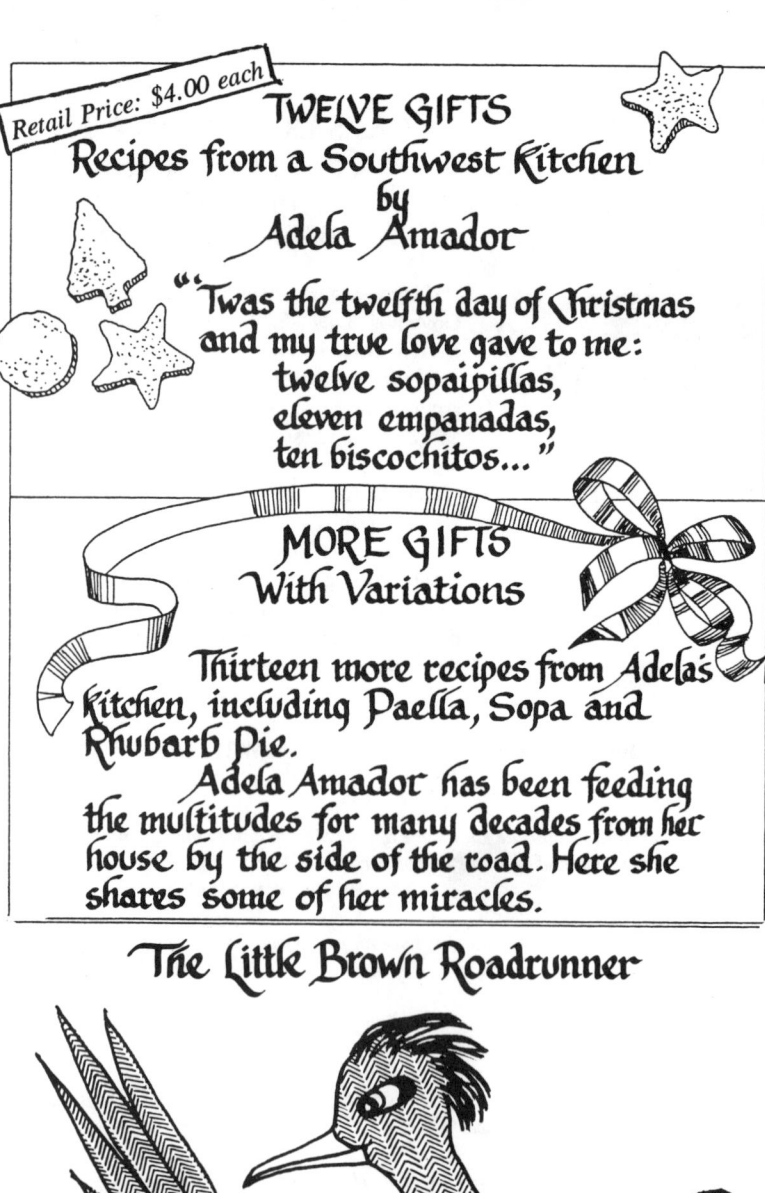

TWELVE GIFTS
Recipes from a Southwest Kitchen
by Adela Amador

"'Twas the twelfth day of Christmas
and my true love gave to me:
  twelve sopaipillas,
  eleven empanadas,
  ten biscochitos..."

MORE GIFTS
With Variations

Thirteen more recipes from Adela's Kitchen, including Paella, Sopa and Rhubarb Pie.

Adela Amador has been feeding the multitudes for many decades from her house by the side of the road. Here she shares some of her miracles.

The Little Brown Roadrunner

THE LITTLE BROWN ROADRUNNER
by Leon Wender
NEW MEXICO's version of THE LITTLE RED HEN